"Can I call you Mommy now?"

little Katie asked hopefully. "'Cause you married my daddy yesterday, so that makes you my new mommy."

Courtney could only stare dumbly at John Gabriel's bright-eyed four-year-old daughter.

John placed a hand on the child's shoulder. "Honey, I really don't think—"

But something warm was stirring within Courtney, filling her heart.

Mommy. Someone wanted to call her Mommy.

She placed her hand on Katie's other shoulder.

And then her eyes met John Gabriel's.

And she had the distinct impression that they were waging a private, primal tug-of-war.

Dear Reader,

Fall is to be savored for all its breathtaking glory—and a spectacular October lineup awaits at Special Edition!

For years, readers have treasured Tracy Sinclair's captivating romances...and October commemorates her fiftieth Silhouette book! To help celebrate this wonderful author's crowning achievement, be sure to check out *The Princess Gets Engaged*—an enthralling romance that finds American tourist Megan Delaney in a royal mess when she masquerades as a princess and falls hopelessly in love with the charming Prince Nicholas.

This month's THAT'S MY BABY! title is by Lois Faye Dyer. *He's Got His Daddy's Eyes* is a poignant reunion story about hope, the enduring power of love and how one little boy works wonders on two broken hearts.

Nonstop romance continues as three veteran authors deliver enchanting stories. Check out award-winning author Marie Ferrarella's adorable tale about mismatched lovers when a blue-blooded heroine hastily marries a blue-collar carpenter in *Wanted: Husband, Will Train*. And what's an amnesiac triplet to do when she washes up on shore and right into the arms of a brooding billionaire? Find out in *The Mysterious Stranger,* when Susan Mallery's engaging TRIPLE TROUBLE series splashes to a finish! Reader favorite Arlene James serves up a tender story about unexpected love in *The Knight, The Waitress and the Toddler*—book four in our FROM BUD TO BLOSSOM promo series.

Finally, October's WOMAN TO WATCH is debut author Lisette Belisle, who unfolds an endearing romance between an innocent country girl and a gruff drifter in *Just Jessie*.

I hope you enjoy these books, and all of the stories to come!

Sincerely,

Tara Gavin, Senior Editor

Please address questions and book requests to:
Silhouette Reader Service
U.S.: 3010 Walden Ave., P.O. Box 1325, Buffalo, NY 14269
Canadian: P.O. Box 609, Fort Erie, Ont. L2A 5X3

MARIE FERRARELLA

WANTED: HUSBAND, WILL TRAIN

Published by Silhouette Books

America's Publisher of Contemporary Romance

To Dr. Darel Benvenuti and Linda.
Thank you
for setting me straight
and putting me on the right path.

SILHOUETTE BOOKS

ISBN 0-373-24132-1

WANTED: HUSBAND, WILL TRAIN

Copyright © 1997 by Marie Rydzynski-Ferrarella

This edition published by arrangement with Harlequin Books S.A.

® and TM are trademarks of Harlequin Books S.A., used under license.
Trademarks indicated with ® are registered in the United States Patent
and Trademark Office, the Canadian Trade Marks Office and in other
countries.

Printed in U.S.A.

Books by Marie Ferrarella

MARIE FERRARELLA

lives in Southern California. She describes herself as the tired mother of two overenergetic children and the contented wife of one wonderful man. The RITA Award-winning author is thrilled to be following her dream of writing full-time.

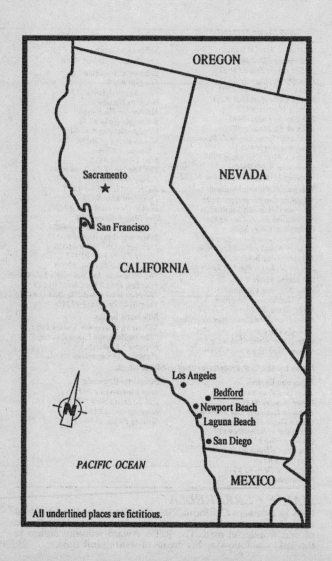

OREGON

NEVADA

Sacramento
★

● San Francisco

CALIFORNIA

N

Los Angeles ●
Bedford
● Newport Beach
Laguna Beach
● San Diego

MEXICO

PACIFIC OCEAN

All underlined places are fictitious.

Chapter One

"Will you be my mommy?"

The soft, melodious voice startled her. She'd thought she was alone. There was no reason to think otherwise. After all, this was her backyard, and her property. Courtney Tamberlaine raised her eyes from the page of the mystery book that she'd found only mildly diverting and looked at the source of the question.

There was a little girl standing before her with hair the color of wheat in the early-morning sunlight and eyes the color of the sky. A little girl of about four or five.

A little girl she didn't know.

Courtney shut her book and swung her legs off the chaise longue. Shading her eyes from the glare of the sun bouncing off the pool, she regarded the child in stunned silence. Who was she and how had she gotten in here?

"Excuse me?"

Suddenly shy, the child dug her hands into the pockets of her pink flower-print overalls. She rocked a little on the balls of her sneakered feet. For the first time, Courtney noticed her complexion. The little girl was incredibly fair. Fair enough to remind Courtney of the china-doll collection she'd owned when she was younger.

"Will you be my mommy?" the child patiently repeated. Shyness gave way to a smile. The small, pink curve seemed to light up everything around her. "You look just like her."

And the little girl didn't look like anyone Courtney knew. "Who are you?"

As far as she was aware, none of the staff had any relatives around that age and there was no way she could have just wandered in off the street. The security alarms along the black wrought-iron fencing would have announced her long before she reached poolside.

"Katie." A deep male voice rumbled behind Courtney. It was stern, though clearly tempered with affection.

Rather than looking embarrassed or frightened, the little girl gave a wide smile as her eyes darted toward the man calling her name.

Just how many people were there wandering around here who she wasn't aware of?

Annoyed, Courtney turned around to see a man walking toward them. A blond, bare-chested, sweaty, bronzed god of a man wearing jeans that were slung low from the weight of a tool belt he had strapped to his hips. For a long moment, all Courtney could do was stare. He looked like every woman's fantasy come true.

Who was that?

Obviously unconcerned about who she was, he gave her a short, polite nod as he took the child's hand in his.

Unaccustomed to being so lightly dismissed, Courtney straightened.

"I'm sorry, she shouldn't be here," the man said, looking down into the small upturned face. There was nothing but patience and love in his eyes. "Katie, what did I tell you about bothering people while I'm working?"

"You said not to." The small face remained undaunted by the gentle reprimand. "But look, Daddy. She looks like Mommy."

Courtney's eyes slid along the lean, muscular torso. His skin, darkened from toiling in the open, gleamed with the sheen of hard labor. Courtney realized that she was holding her breath and exhaled slowly. Mommy, whoever she was, was a very lucky woman.

Something—she couldn't quite put her finger on what—flashed through his eyes as they flickered over her at the child's behest. In the middle of the warmest day in July in recent California history, Courtney felt a chill wrap itself around her.

"No, she doesn't look like Mommy." His manner was patient. It was evident that he cared for the little girl a great deal. But the words themselves were ground out.

Maybe Mommy wasn't all that lucky at that, Courtney amended.

"But the picture, Daddy," Katie insisted, unwilling to be put off so easily. Confused, she looked up at her father. "She looks like the picture in your big white book."

Entertaining though all this was, Courtney still didn't have an answer to her question. Who were these people and what were they doing on her property?

Courtney rose slowly from her lounge chair, tugging

at the slim string of her bikini to move it back into place. She tucked her book under her arm. Aware of the impression she generated, she watched the man's face and noted with pleasure that an appreciative glint lit the man's eyes, though his expression never changed.

As his eyes met hers, he turned abruptly and began to walk off, his daughter's hand securely held in his. Courtney watched the hilt of the hammer attached to his belt swing rhythmically against his hip like a metronome moving in slow time.

She blinked, astounded that they could just come and go like this.

"Wait a minute," Courtney called after them. "Just who are you?"

The man stopped and turned around, still holding his daughter's hand, though she seemed eager to run back to her for a closer look.

"My name's John Gabriel. I was hired by someone named Sloan to renovate the guest house. This is my daughter, Katie."

"Oh." With deliberate, measured steps, Courtney crossed to where they were standing. Gabriel, she noted, bemused, kept his eyes on her face.

She vaguely recalled asking Sloan to see about getting the guest house a face-lift. Confident in the man's competence, she'd left the details entirely in the old butler's hands. She wondered if the man Sloan hired worked half as well as he looked.

"That means you're actually working for me." Courtney put out her hand. "I'm Courtney Tamberlaine. This is my house."

John took the hand she offered and shook it. "House" was hardly an adequate word for the place. It was more like a museum, he thought. Far too big to be thought of as comfortable or a home, at least as far as his tastes ran. But the spacious design was architecturally pleasing and he could admire the structure without actually liking what had been done with it.

"Nice place," he allowed. The woman was still holding his hand. He was aware of the gleeful look in Katie's eyes. Though it gladdened his heart to see his daughter happy, he didn't want the wrong impression flowering in her young mind. "I'm being paid by the hour."

Courtney inclined her head. Another man in this situation would have said something witty in an attempt to impress her. Maybe he wasn't capable of witty. Maybe what she saw was all there was. A gorgeous outer shell with no interesting matter inside.

She withdrew her hand. "Then I'd better let you work." Turning, Courtney began to walk away, confident that he was watching her.

But when she glanced over her shoulder, she saw that Gabriel was busy shepherding his daughter back toward the guest house. He wasn't even looking in her direction. Mildly miffed, Courtney shrugged and pulled open the French doors. She'd had enough of sun for one day, anyway.

With a toss of her head that was meant to totally blot out the existence of the annoying laborer, she was halfway across the family room before she was aware that there was someone in the room with her.

"So, is that what they're wearing, or should I say *not* wearing, on the Riviera these days?"

Courtney didn't have to look. The voice was all too familiar, ingrained in her brain with a multitude of memories that dated back to the earliest ones of her childhood.

Throwing open her arms, she crossed to her oldest

friend. "Mandy! When did you get in?" Courtney hadn't expected her to be back for another week at the very least.

Engulfed in the embrace, Miranda Calhoun returned it with feeling. "This morning." She sighed dramatically for effect. "The flight from Athens was an absolute endurance test."

Courtney reached for the short green robe she'd left on the back of the sofa. "In first class?" She slipped her arms through the sleeves as she laughed. "Yeah, I'll just bet."

Mandy arranged herself on the sofa, spreading out her wide, ice blue skirt. It showed off her tan. "What first class? I flew in Louis's jet. It was Louis who was the endurance test." Brown eyes just a shade darker than her hair snapped with a joke that was not to remain a secret for long. "He wants to marry me."

Men always wanted to marry Mandy. She was as diminutive as Courtney was statuesque. It gave her a waif-like quality that made men want to take care of her. The appearance belied an iron independent streak that was a mile wide.

Courtney leaned against the arm of the sofa. She knew the answer even before she asked, but allowed Mandy her moment. "And?"

"And?" Tidy brows drew together. "What am I, crazy? I don't want to be the third Mrs. Norville when I finally get married. I don't want to be the third anything." She smoothed out a wave in her skirt. "When I get married, I want to be the first Mrs. Something-or-other." Tilting her head like a robin pondering the best strategy to use to coax a worm from its hole, she studied her best friend's face. "Speaking of married—"

Courtney rose abruptly from her perch, a warning look in her eyes. "Don't start."

The tone told her everything. Mandy couldn't believe it. "You mean you haven't begun yet?"

Courtney carelessly shrugged her shoulders beneath the robe. A strap dipped down and she pushed it back into place. "Begun what?"

Mandy waved her hands vaguely in the air, like a sorcerer conjuring up a spell. For lack of a better word, she retorted, "Proceedings."

"Proceedings," Courtney repeated. A small smile curved the corners of her mouth. Proceedings. A euphemism for wedding arrangements. "A little difficult without a husband-to-be in the picture."

Mandy shook her head. "Well, you'd better reframe your picture, Courtney, or you're going to be out on the street corner, selling flowers in—what, thirty days?"

Courtney thought of the date on her calendar. "Twenty-eight, but who's counting?"

"You should be. Hell, Court, talk about being in denial. Anyone else would have already lined up the hall by now." Mandy frowned. "Why do you think your father did that, anyway?"

It had been something he had threatened to do all along, but Courtney hadn't really believed he would. Not until he'd died and the will had been read. Even now, she couldn't believe that there wasn't a way around it. Her father wouldn't have backed her against the wall like that. She'd always felt that there had to be some loophole somewhere, if only she could appeal to their family lawyer.

"I think Dad believed he was teaching me something about values." Courtney shrugged the matter away. She didn't really want to discuss it. "I don't know. All I do know is that that clause is ridiculous and there's no way Edwin Parsons is going to hold me to it." Her eyes met Mandy's, which were filled with skepticism. "He can't. He's a family friend." *Her* friend, in a manner of speaking, although the bonds of friendship had been forged between the thin, humorless man and her father.

The Tamberlaines and the Calhouns were both represented by the same firm. "He is also the family lawyer," Mandy reminded her pointedly. "Daddy says he's unreproachable." It was why her own family dealt exclusively with the wizened lawyer and why, Mandy knew, Courtney's father had, as well.

It had taken Courtney time to reconcile herself to the fact that her father had meant well. But she couldn't bring herself to believe that she could actually be all but disinherited, except for a small yearly allowance, if she didn't follow the letter of the clause. It all sounded far too medieval.

But Mandy was right. Time was growing short. She needed to be assured that everything would be all right if she wasn't standing in front of an altar within the next four weeks, saying words no one meant anymore.

She set her mouth. "Every man can be bought."

Mandy's eyes widened as she straightened on the sofa. "You'd try to bribe him?"

Bribery had such an ugly sound to it. Courtney didn't want to think in terms of ugly. Not when the matter was connected to something that had to do with her father. He'd been a stubborn old man, but she'd loved no one more and she missed him dearly.

Courtney gave a short, noncommittal nod. "Only as a last measure."

"With what?" Mandy hooted. "In case you've forgotten, most of your money is locked up in a trust. And

Eddie Parsons has the keys, so to speak.'' She grinned. No one would have dared call the lawyer Eddie to his face, except maybe Courtney. "No, if you don't want your money scattered to the winds and five hundred charities, you'd better find yourself a man, Courtney. And quick.''

Courtney was acutely aware of the fact that at almost thirty she still wasn't allowed to manage the sum total of her wealth, thanks to her father and what he deemed was his wisdom. "Finding a man isn't the problem.'' She knew a great many men, all of whom would have loved to be associated with the Tamberlaine money. Hammering out an acceptable prenuptial agreement would probably take longer than the allotted time she supposedly had. Besides, none met her father's requirement: a hard-working man from a working-class background. "It's the marrying part I don't like. No one can dictate to me.''

Mandy grinned. Something beyond the French doors caught her eye and she turned her head to get a better look. "Your father obviously can, even if it is from the Great Beyond.''

That was true enough, although she didn't like it. "I suppose he thought it was a good thing when he did it.'' She knew better. It was a hopelessly outdated idea. "But just because Mother was a waitress before he married her doesn't mean that I have to go to a local thrift shop to pick out a husband.''

"Why not advertise?'' Humor twisted Mandy's lips as she spread her hands in the air, as if to frame the ad. "Wanted: Husband, Will Train.'' She winked. "That's in case his 'rough' background proves to be too rough for your tastes.''

The humor in the situation escaped Courtney. "I don't like being forced into anything."

There was a man by Courtney's guest house, Mandy realized. A gorgeous half-naked man who, if he had any pity on the world at large, wouldn't have stopped at shedding his clothing when he removed his shirt.

"Things could always be worse," Mandy mumbled, only half listening to Courtney's response. She rose to her knees, watching the man bend over as he took measure of something or other. Mandy almost swallowed her tongue. Eyes bright, she looked at Courtney. "Hey, who *is* that gorgeous hunk?"

"Hmm?" Preoccupied, Courtney stepped over to see what Mandy was staring at. She might have known. "Oh, him." She waved a hand dismissively. "Sloan hired him to fix up the guest house."

Leaning against the back of the sofa, Mandy propped her head up against her hands and continued staring. "Wow. Can Sloan get him for me?"

An uneasiness was beginning to set in. Courtney was getting a strong feeling that maybe Mandy was right for a change. Maybe Parsons wouldn't relent.

"You don't have a guest house," she murmured, distracted. She crossed to the desk and pulled the telephone closer. No time like the present.

"What guest house?" Mandy spared Courtney one quick look over her shoulder before she returned her gaze to the man beyond the pool. "I mean for me. He's absolutely beautiful."

Mandy had exhaled the last word as if she were uttering a prayer. Courtney glanced up and took another look at Gabriel. She shrugged. "In a raw sort of way."

Mandy looked up at her friend, obviously puzzled. "And that would be a bad thing because...?"

Mandy always went for the ones without depth. Courtney shook her head, terminating the discussion.

"Never mind." She tapped out the number to Parsons's office. It was a small firm, with only two other
partners, both junior, and Parsons at the head. He was
at a place in his life now where he could pick and choose
who he represented. "Mr. Parsons, please." Courtney
sighed as the woman on the other end tried to put her
off. "No, I won't leave a message. This is Courtney
Tamberlaine. I need to speak to him. Now. Thank you."

Courtney waited for Parsons to come on the line. She
toyed with the wire and looked toward Mandy. The
woman looked as if she was in a trance. Curious, Courtney followed her transfixed gaze. Gabriel had just moved
into view again. Because of the way the sun hit, she was
aware more than ever of the sheen of perspiration on his
body.

As was Mandy. She sighed, looking up at Courtney.
"Glows, doesn't he?"

Courtney moved away from the view. "That's
sweat."

"Yeah." Mandy wiggled farther into her cushion, as
if in her mind she had already found a way to share that
dampened state with him. "I know."

"You're hopeless," Courtney murmured. Although,
she could see what the attraction was this time, she
added silently. He was good-looking, if somewhat rude.

Courtney's mind snapped to attention as the gentle
classical music abruptly stopped on the other end of the
line. "Mr. Parsons? Yes, this is Courtney Tamberlaine.
About my father's will—" Courtney was prepared to
roll right over him until she stated—and got—what she
wanted.

The Oxford-educated voice broke in as if she wasn't speaking. "Yes, Miss Tamberlaine?"

From the steely tone, Courtney knew this was going to be an uphill fight. Well, so be it. She was up to the challenge. There was a hell of a prize at stake, one she wanted without having to expand her family of one.

Damn it, it was her heritage, her due. When he was alive, her father had lavished her with attention and gifts far beyond anything she could imagine. Why, in death, had he made life so difficult for her?

There was no room for idle chitchat. Taking a breath, she plunged into the heart of it. "You're not seriously going to hold me to that clause, are you?"

She could have sworn she heard mild amusement on the other end. Parsons might have even smiled. Now there would have been a rare sight, she thought dourly.

"The one that states if you're not married by your thirtieth birthday to a hard-working man of the middle class your money, except for a generous allowance, reverts to a number of charities your father enumerated?"

It was hard not to grit her teeth together. "Yes, that one."

"I most certainly am."

Yes, he was definitely smiling. Perhaps even grinning. Courtney addressed him in her most formidable tone. "Mr. Parsons—"

There was no indication that it fazed him the way it did others when she used it. "It's not *my* will, Miss Tamberlaine, it's your father's, and it is my sworn duty as his lawyer to uphold it."

There had to be a way around this. "If I could have an extension—"

There was a pause and a rustle of paper, as if he was perusing the will to double-check details. As if it wasn't indelibly etched into his brain, the way every other scrap of paper he'd ever put a pen to seemed to be, she thought, annoyed.

Finally, he answered. "There was no mention of extensions."

She wanted to be indulged, not patronized. Courtney tried again, attempting to appeal to his sense of fair play. "You can't expect me to run out and marry the first laborer I find, do you?"

Courtney saw the wide grin on Mandy's face as the other woman pointed toward the French doors. Courtney turned her back on Mandy.

"I haven't the right to expect anything, Miss Tamberlaine," Parsons's accented voice carefully enunciated in her ear. "Your father, however, having made you aware of the terms of the will before he died, did have the right to expect you to have found someone by now. It isn't as if this could come as a surprise to you at this point."

The pompous bastard. Courtney struggled to bridle her frustration. "No, but I thought you would be reasonable about this."

She might as well have been arguing with a wall for all the impression she made. "I am the soul of reasonableness, Miss Tamberlaine. However, it states here in black and white—"

She knew damn well what it stated and didn't need to have it read to her. "Fine."

With an uncustomary display of temper, Courtney slammed the receiver down into the cradle. It bounced off. Muttering, she replaced it a second time.

Now what?

"No luck?" Mandy guessed, tongue in cheek. With regret, she forced herself to tear her eyes away from the

view. Her neck was beginning to ache. Watching Courtney pace around the room, Mandy slowly rotated her
head from side to side.

Courtney slanted her a look to see if Mandy was attempting to be funny. It didn't matter. Courtney waved
a hand at the telephone.

"He's an unmovable old bastard." Granted, she
hadn't tried to bribe him, but Mandy was right. That
wouldn't have worked, anyway.

What would it have cost the old grump to let her slide
for a while?

Mandy settled back against the cushions. "He's only
carrying out your father's wishes."

Courtney frowned. She knew that. But it didn't make
things any easier to cope with. And she had to blame
someone. She didn't like the thought of railing against
her father.

"You're no help." She spun around on her heel,
bringing the challenge to Mandy's feet. "How am I supposed to find the love of my life in twenty-eight days?"
She threw up her hands. "Where am I supposed to look?
In the Yellow Pages under _L?_"

Mandy suddenly smiled. "How about in your own
backyard?"

She was having a crisis and Mandy was still salivating
over the help! Courtney blew out a breath. "His name
is John Gage or Gabriel or something like that. You want
a date?"

Mandy spared the man one last look, but he had
moved out of view again. "I wish. No, I meant for you."

Courtney stopped pacing and looked at Mandy. "For
me, what?" Courtney asked slowly. She couldn't imagine that Mandy actually meant....

Sometimes Courtney could be positively obtuse,

Mandy thought. Excited, she got off the sofa. "Your working man." Gripping Courtney by the arms, she turned her friend toward the French doors. "The kind of guy your father wanted you to find."

Courtney pulled away as she rolled her eyes. "Oh please—besides, he's married."

"Oh." Disappointment fairly dripped from the single word. Mandy cast a last hopeful look toward the object of the conversation. "You're sure?"

"He has a daughter," Courtney informed her tersely. "As a matter of fact, she just asked me to be her mommy." Courtney replayed the scene at the pool in her mind. Her eyes shifted to Mandy. "Why would she ask me to be her mommy?"

Mandy shrugged. "She doesn't like the one she has?"

That wasn't it. Courtney drew her bottom lip in between her teeth, thinking. "No, she said something about my looking like her. Like her picture."

It was all the clue Mandy needed. "That means she doesn't have the genuine article!" Eyes bright with excitement, she grasped Courtney's arm again. "Which means Mr. Tool-Belt-with-the-gorgeous-hips is either divorced or widowed." She snapped her fingers. "Bingo."

Sometimes she didn't think there were any planes landing in Mandy's airport. "What bingo?"

Courtney was like a horse that had to be led to water and then splashed with it. Mandy curbed her impatience. "As in you win the prize." She gestured toward the French doors and what she clearly regarded as the perfect specimen of manhood just beyond. "Him."

Frozen in place, Courtney felt numb. "You're not seriously suggesting—?"

"Yes, I am. Very seriously," Mandy insisted. Her expression bore her out. "He's the answer to your dilemma, not to mention most women's dreams.'' She eyed her best friend. ''Unless you have any better ideas?''

Courtney turned away from the view of the backyard. And Gabriel. She refused to look at Mandy. Feeling suddenly weary and at a loss, she headed toward the bar. She normally didn't drink, and then only after five. But all rules were broken sometimes.

''Mandy, we've been friends since childhood. Otherwise, I'd seriously suggest to your father that he have you committed.'' Courtney took out a glass, her hand on a crystal decanter. It remained poised there.

Mandy laid her hand over her friend's. When Courtney looked into her eyes, she saw only compassion there. ''C'mon, Court, you're not thinking. It'll be a business proposition. An arranged marriage. A guy like that's got to have needs—''

Courtney laughed shortly, but there was no humor in the sound. When it came down to it, she was sure that John Gabriel was just like any other man she'd met. Just out for himself and his own pleasures. ''Yes, I know.''

For a second, a foolish grin crossed Mandy's mouth. Then she roused herself. ''No, I mean monetary ones. He's a single father working odd jobs. These are expensive times. Maybe he'd like to give the kid a few more things than he can afford—like college.'' She shrugged. ''Make him a deal. Look, you've got everything to gain and nothing to lose.''

Courtney rolled the idea over in her mind. It was absolutely insane, and yet...what choice did she have? And at least here, if she made up the terms, she would be in the driver's seat.

''In a crazy way, I suppose you do have a point. I'm certainly not going to find true love in twenty-eight days and I resent being painted into a corner like that." Hands braced on the knob of both doors, she pulled them open. A ripple of excitement telegraphed itself through her. "Okay. Here goes."

Mandy stopped her before she could get any further.

"What?" Courtney paused, puzzled. Wasn't this what Mandy wanted her to do?

"Take off the coverup," Mandy urged. "Let him see what he'll be getting."

He had already seen her without the robe and hadn't thought her worth a second look, Courtney thought, a little petulantly. She lifted her chin. His loss—although it actually would make things less complicated.

"He's not going to be getting anything except a check," she told Mandy.

But she did manage to undo the knot at her waist as she sauntered out. A corner of robe slipped from her shoulder before she reached him.

"Mr. Gabriel." When he didn't respond, Courtney raised her voice. He was hammering too loud to hear. But the little girl came running over to her. That caught his attention and he turned around.

His eyes were amazingly green, she thought. Even at this distance. For the first time, Courtney felt a little less confident than she was comfortable with. "Mr. Gabriel?"

John hooked the hammer on his belt as if he were a gunfighter putting away his weapon. "Yes?"

She was unaware of moistening her lips with the tip of her tongue before she answered. But he wasn't.

"I have a proposition for you."

Chapter Two

Katie furrowed her brow until her bright blue eyes became tiny glittering slits outlined in dark velvet lashes. Confused, she turned toward her foremost authority on absolutely everything. "What's a 'pop-o-zshion,' Daddy?"

John smiled at his little girl. Like a sponge, he thought with pride. Katie wanted to know everything, understand everything. There were times when he just had to stop, stand back and focus on the thought that this precious being had been placed into his life, given to him like a gift. And he had done absolutely nothing to deserve her. The very thought left him in a state of awe.

He placed a firm, gentling hand on the small shoulder, as if to anchor his daughter in place. His gaze had the same effect on Courtney. It all but mortared her to the gray-blue and pink pavers that had been so painstakingly laid into the patio.

What was he thinking? she wondered. There was no way to tell. His expression was chiseled out of stone. Only his eyes testified to his human state. They became warmer whenever he turned them toward his daughter.

John took assessment of the woman before him, only mildly curious about what she had in mind. It was his experience that people who didn't work for a living, who didn't have to worry about bills piling up, had way too much time on their hands. What they found interesting, he rarely did.

"A proposition is what people call suggestions they feel other people can't refuse," he explained to his daughter.

He was almost mocking her as he said it, Courtney realized. Now she could see what he was thinking. Those gorgeous, wide, bronzed shoulders had a chip on them. She couldn't begin to guess at its origin, but it almost seemed to have something to do with her. She thought of abandoning the whole ridiculous idea, but then she thought of her other options.

There weren't any.

She was in a corner—never mind that it was partially her own cavalier doing. Unless something better occurred to her between now and her birthday, this was it.

And "it" didn't look very flexible.

Courtney could feel her spine stiffening, her body girding up for a challenge. *Damn you, Daddy, is this what you wanted? To have me grabbing hold of some sweaty laborer with a drill bit just because you thought that someone who worked for a living would have the right values for me? I have all the right values, Daddy. I don't need that firm hand guiding me that you were always talking about.*

This was no time to carry on a silent argument with her father. She had some tall convincing to do.

"Your father's half-right—" Courtney thought for a moment, trying to recall the girl's name. "Katie." Courtney smiled at the delicate little face. "It's more of a business deal where both people involved get something they want." She doubted that Katie could understand what she was saying, but it was the best she could do. The last time she'd talked to a child, she had been one.

Courtney glanced toward Gabriel. His eyes were polite, but impersonal. And very distant. Apparently she'd scored no points for talking to his daughter.

Katie was right, John mused. There were similarities between Diane and the Tamberlaine woman. It went beyond the physical. She was very sure of herself, sure of getting what she wanted, just as Diane had been. He remembered a time he would have given his late ex-wife everything. Until he discovered that she wanted more.

"And what is it that you want, Miss Tamberlaine?"

There were nice, slow ways to work up to her subject. Diplomatic ways. Given time, Courtney could have framed this discussion artfully. But she didn't have that luxury. She'd spent it.

Courtney drew a breath, feeling oddly unsteady for a moment, as if she were about to take a dive off a very steep cliff. "What I want, Gabriel, is a husband."

There were a lot of things he might have expected her to say, but this was not even remotely close to any of them. John's hand slid off Katie's shoulder as he stared at the woman standing in front of him. He couldn't have heard her right. "And you'd like me to build you one?"

The superior look in his eyes had temporarily receded. She rather liked that.

"No, I'd like you to be one."

It was a joke, of course, but the punch line seemed a long time in coming. He waited and so did she. Finally, he said incredulously, "To you." It wasn't even a question, it was an absurd statement. One he fully expected her to laugh off.

Courtney was aware that the little girl was staring at her. "To me."

Courtney Tamberlaine didn't appear to be an unstable woman—arrogant, perhaps, but not unstable. Obviously, she had to be. Either that, or she had a very twisted sense of humor. "Did I miss something? Why are you asking me to be—?"

"*Are* you going to be my mommy?"

Katie had edged her father out of the way and was tugging on the end of Courtney's robe. It had slipped completely off one shoulder.

Oh, no, Katie wasn't going to be pulled into this woman's bizarre game, whatever it was. John squeezed Katie's shoulder lightly, moving her toward him. "No, she is not going to be your mommy, Katie. I think Ms. Tamberlaine must be a little muddled and has her months mixed up." The look in his eyes warned Courtney to drop the charade. "This is July, not April first."

He was annoyed with her, Courtney thought. The realization nudged uneasiness into anger. Who the hell did he think he was, to be annoyed with her? She was the one with the problem, not him. Hell, she was about to make him a rich man through absolutely no merit of his own, except that he'd had the good fortune of being in the right place at the right time.

"I never get muddled," she informed him icily, then forced herself to smile. She was negotiating, she reminded herself. "Will you join me on the patio for a glass of lemonade? I'd like to explain this to you. Slowly.''

She'd deliberately enunciated the last word. Her point was not lost on him. Ms. Tamberlaine obviously thought he was slow-witted because he was working with his hands. Pride almost managed to get the best of him. The same pride he'd harbored as he'd worked his way through college, earning an engineering degree while re- modeling other people's kitchens.

That was how he'd met Diane, building new cabinets for her mother. He'd been twenty at the time, and had mistaken aloofness for breeding. He was older now and knew better.

John looked back at the guest house. He worked ac- cording to a strict schedule he set up for himself. And she was wasting his time.

Taking Katie's hand, he nodded toward the structure and began edging away. He noticed that Katie wasn't eager to follow. ''As I said earlier, you're paying me by the hour and—''

Courtney was in no mood to be put off by excuses. ''Then I get to decide how you spend your time earning that money.''

A dark blond brow arched over eyes as green as clo- vers growing wild in the field. ''Within reason.''

Courtney's smile widened as her eyes swept over Ka- tie. ''I am always reasonable.''

John doubted that a woman like Courtney Tamber- laine was reasonable unless she absolutely had to be, but it was her dollar and if she wanted to spend it talking to him under a striped canopy, sipping lemonade, it was her call. Besides, Katie had been behaved for most of the morning. She deserved a break far more than he did.

He nodded and gestured toward the patio. ''All right.

Let's see you explain your request and make it sound reasonable.''

Something distant and unformed warned Courtney to take her proposal off the table, turn tail and run now, while she still had the chance. Stubbornness prevented her.

As soon as he released her hand, Katie shifted over to the lady who looked so much like the picture she'd seen of her mommy. A smile beaming on her face, Katie confided, ''I love lemonade. It makes my lips tingle.''

Tingle. Courtney bet Katie's father probably knew a thing or two about making a woman tingle. Those hands looked as if they knew their way around more than just carpenter's tools.

The thought occurred to her that she might be getting more than she bargained for. But then, she'd always been up to any challenge sent her way. Keeping him in line would be just another challenge.

She didn't doubt her abilities for a minute.

Courtney placed an arm around the little girl's shoulders, shepherding her toward the patio table. She was struck by how delicate and fragile the little girl seemed. ''You can have as much as you like.''

''Thank you.''

Courtney knew several adults who weren't as articulate or as polite as Katie. She looked at Gabriel over her shoulder. ''How old is she?''

Before John could answer, Katie proudly held up four fingers, wiggling them for emphasis. ''Four. I'm four years old.''

Although her size made her seem even younger than that, she had almost an adult bearing about her. Probably got that from her father, Courtney thought.

''She's very well-spoken for four.'' Courtney cer-

tainly found her much easier to talk to and like than her
father.

His uncle and aunt, the only parents he had ever
known, had always talked at him, not to him. John had
grown up feeling as if he were only part of the furnishing
in their three room apartment, not part of their lives.
He'd vowed when she was born that Katie would never
feel like that.

"I don't see any reason to talk down to her."

His answer was said with feeling. She felt as if they
were sparring partners, feeling each other out. "Very
admirable of you."

She saw the way Gabriel looked at Katie as he moved
her chair in for her. In a way, Gabriel reminded her a
little of her own father. An unexpected sting of nostalgia
pricked her as she remembered the way Alexander Tamberlaine had always doted on her, hovering protectively
as her mother laughed and said that she wasn't made of
glass.

No she wasn't, but she had shattered anyway when he
died. Yet she had always managed to turn a laughing,
carefree face to the world.

She'd fooled everyone.

No one really knew what went on in her head. Not
even her father. If he had, he would have trusted her
judgment and she wouldn't be wrestling with this damn
albatross he had hung around her neck.

*As if I didn't have enough brains to eventually pick a
decent husband.*

Courtney took her own chair and was surprised when
Gabriel helped her with hers. "Nice manners."

He wondered if she felt that he needed her approval.
"I bathe regularly, too."

Amusement lifted the corners of her mouth. "Another

commendable quality." Courtney turned to see if Sloan or Angela, the maid, were anywhere within view. She saw Sloan passing the French doors in the library and signaled for him to come out.

Katie's mouth dropped open as she watched Everett Sloan walk out onto the patio toward their table. Dressed in black livery—as his post, his training and his heritage demanded—Sloan, at a very thin six foot six, was an imposing sight.

"Who's that?" she whispered, shifting in her seat to be closer to her father.

Courtney felt herself smiling. She could remember having the same reaction to Sloan. She'd been no older than Katie when the butler had first come to work for her father.

"This is Sloan, Katie. He'll bring you that lemonade you want." Courtney turned to look at him as Sloan approached. "Won't you, Sloan?"

"Right away, Miss." The somber, impassive face gave way to a slight smile as he looked down at the little girl. "Will that be three lemonades, Miss?"

Courtney glanced toward Gabriel. "Unless you'd like something stronger?"

John had a feeling that he might need something stronger by the time she was finished, but there was still a lot to do. Besides, he had Katie to think of. "Lemonade will be fine."

She nodded at Sloan, who began to retreat. Struck by a thought, she held up her hand. "Wait." Courtney looked at Katie. "Any particular color lemonade you'd prefer?"

There wasn't even a moment's hesitation. "Pink. It's my favorite color."

She couldn't have said it with more confidence than

if she were ordering wine in an expensive restaurant. Amused, Courtney impulsively covered Katie's hand with her own. "Pink it is." She raised her eyes to her butler. "Sloan?"

"Pink it shall be." With a slight inclination of his salt-and-pepper-fringed head, Sloan withdrew to grant the little girl's request.

Out of the corner of her eye, Courtney could see Mandy watching them from the library. Though it was too far away to see her expression, Courtney had no doubts that her best friend was dying to be included in this discussion.

She could feel Gabriel's eyes on her, practically penetrating her mind. But if he was curious, he managed his curiosity well. He was waiting for her to pick her time.

Damn, why was there this flutter in the pit of her stomach? This was no different than buying a sailboat, or choosing a new car. And ultimately, except for outward appearances, it was even less binding.

Composing herself, Courtney folded her hands before her on the table and studied the man sitting opposite her. He looked even more virile, more masculine than before. She had to concentrate not to let her imagination drift.

"Are you seeing anyone, John?"

"That's personal, Ms. Tamberlaine." Was she continuing with this joke? Just what was her game? She hadn't really seemed interested in him earlier and she wasn't really interested in him now, not the way Diane had been, hanging around, trying to strike up conversations with him as he worked, trying to get him to notice her. But Diane had been nineteen and full of pride at her nubile, sleek little body. This one had something else on her mind. And somehow she seemed to think he fit into it.

He was too busy to be the source of amusement for a rich, spoiled heiress.

"Then you are seeing someone?"

There was no one in his life. There was no time for anyone but Katie. She needed him far more than he needed to feel the warmth of a woman's soft body beside him at night. "I said it was personal," he replied evenly. "I *didn't* answer your question one way or another."

Impatience drummed at Courtney. She held it in check. Letting it get the better of her wasn't going to help the situation. "No, you didn't, but I do need an answer. Are you seeing anyone, or involved with anyone, at the moment?"

She certainly wasn't shy, he thought, almost amused by her question. But then, he doubted that she'd ever found the occasion to be shy. She probably utilized everything she had to her advantage. There was no doubt in his mind that the stunning figure housed a very shallow woman.

He opened his mouth to answer, but Sloan picked that time to return. The butler slipped three tall glasses from the tray just as unobtrusively as he had entered and placed one before each of them on the table.

With an exclamation of glee, Katie wrapped her hands around the frosty glass. She giggled as she brought it down to her level. Sloan had thought to put a straw into hers and she covered it eagerly with her small mouth.

Courtney saw John eyeing his daughter and could almost feel the breath that he was holding as he waited to see if the maneuver was a successful one.

He cared about the little girl, Courtney thought again. Really cared. A man who felt that way about his daughter couldn't be all bad. It made her feel a little better about the insanity she was about to undertake.

"So," Courtney pressed, "*are* you involved with any-one?"

He had to admit that he was more curious than he should be.

"And if I said I wasn't...?"

Yes! He was free. Gabriel didn't strike her as the type to play games. And if he was lying, Courtney had the feeling that Katie would have contradicted him with her gentle innocence and mentioned a woman's name. Courtney breathed a sigh of relief.

Suddenly aware that he was watching her, she released the remainder of it slowly. "Then I would elaborate on my proposition."

He hoped that whatever she had to say, she would remember that there was a child present. "Go ahead, I'm listening."

Courtney had always taken pride in not being afraid to face anything. The meek were left behind, ignored, abandoned. She had never been meek and, as far as she recalled, she'd never really felt awkward.

Until now.

Her palms were actually damp, she realized with a touch of wonder and disgust.

It had to do with the man's eyes. His eyes, such a beautiful green, were looking straight into her. Delving into her. Making her lose her train of thought and con-fusing her as if she were some unsophisticated schoolgirl instead of a well-traveled woman who could cite friends on both sides of the Atlantic and Pacific.

For reasons she could not put into words, none of that seemed to matter right now.

Maybe a little background *was* necessary. She needed to arouse his sympathy. If he possessed any. "My father placed great store in the working class."

Next, she was probably going to tell him that dear old dad made a point of inviting a blue collar worker to share Thanksgiving dinner with them every year. John was well acquainted with the type. He felt the edge of his temper sharpening. "Nice of him."

That chip of his was growing right before her eyes. Courtney set her mouth, determined. She was never more her father's daughter than when she felt the odds stacked against her.

Ignoring the sarcasm in Gabriel's voice, she continued, "He was a very nice man, if a little eccentric at the end."

The end. That meant the man had probably passed on. John still didn't see what any of this had to do with him. "And you're going to get to that part."

"Yes." She'd snapped the word out before she could stop herself. Now she probably came off sounding like a shrew, but it was only because she felt herself backed into a corner. "My father wanted to have me marry someone from the working class before I was thirty."

It took all kinds. Diane's family had wanted her to have nothing to do with him; they had talked against him until she had "come to her senses" and divorced him. Obviously, Tamberlaine's father had had a different frame of mind. But why was she telling him this? With her looks, he couldn't imagine her having any difficulty attracting likely candidates.

Although he could see where her mouth might get in the way.

It was getting late. "I don't see what this has to do with me."

Maybe he was thicker than she thought. "I'm going to be thirty next month."

What might have passed for a smile lightly creased his lips. "Happy birthday."

Her eyes held his. Was he being sarcastic? "It would be a great deal happier if I were married."

She couldn't possibly mean... John waited for her to say something that made sense. "And—?"

Courtney leaned over the table, for the moment shutting out the child who was absorbing every word. "And I'm prepared to offer you a sum of money if you'll be my husband."

"Then you *are* serious?"

Unfortunately. "Very."

John pushed back his chair, the legs scraping along the concrete. "Lady, I don't know what you've been sipping besides lemonade, but this is getting far too weird for me."

Courtney felt a sudden onslaught of panic overtake her. What if he was her last opportunity to fulfill that ridiculous requirement?

"Wait!"

Gabriel looked at her expectantly and she hurried to continue, silently damning both him and her father. "My father's will specifies that if I'm not married by the time I'm thirty, the bulk of his money is to be distributed among his favorite charities."

"And you don't qualify." It was hard for him to feel sympathy.

She shrugged. Her father had had good intentions, she supposed. And he wasn't heartless. "I would get a specified allowance."

Which was probably twice as much as he'd gotten to see in a good year when he'd been working as an engineer. "That's more than most people have guaranteed."

If he was trying to make her feel guilty about wanting more of her own money, he wasn't succeeding. "I am aware of that," she replied evenly, "but I don't want to lose the house."

It was far too big a house, anyway, John thought. He could have lived very comfortably in the guest house, with room to spare—before the renovations. But he knew that people like Courtney were too rigid and too self-serving to adjust.

"That's life, Ms. Tamberlaine. We all lose something." He shoved in his chair with an air of finality. "I'm afraid I can't help you."

The clod. He wasn't even hearing her out. Courtney rose quickly to her feet. Her robe caught on the edge of the chair and she tugged it free. "It would be strictly business."

Though the smile on his lips widened, it was completely without feeling. "My first marriage turned out to be that way. I'd rather not have to endure a repeat performance."

"Don't you understand? It wouldn't be a real marriage—"

He glanced at Katie and lowered his voice. "Neither was my first one, as it turned out."

She played her trump card. "Isn't there something you want for yourself?" She gestured toward Katie. "For your daughter?"

The expression on his face warned her to keep Katie out of it. "People can't be bought."

Her hands tightened around the back of the chair as she struggled to keep the angry, desperate note out of her voice. "I'm not buying you, I'm renting you. For two years." Momentarily succeeding in catching his interest, she hurried on. "You're how old?"

"Thirty-one." What did that have to do with any-thing?

She inclined her head. "In two years you'll be thirty-three—and two hundred thousand dollars richer." She watched his face, expecting to see capitulation as well as surprised pleasure. To her amazement, she saw nei-ther.

"Why are you so desperate?" It didn't make any sense to him. "A woman who looks like you could have any one of a number of men."

"If that's a compliment, thank you." She doubted he meant it that way. He was probably one of those people who resented anyone with more money than he had. "But the men I have met have all been far too dazzled by my father's money to really see me. I don't think it would have mattered to any one of them if I looked like Victor Hugo's bell ringer." She paused. The reference was probably out of his league. "That's—"

She really did know how to talk down to a person, didn't she? "I know who that is, Ms. Tamberlaine. I minored in literature."

Surprise highlighted her features. She looked at his tool belt. "You went to college?"

Her reaction was almost comical. "Third in my class. UCLA. Engineering."

Then why—? Courtney reconnoitered. "I didn't mean to insult you."

She'd done a damn good job of it, though. "Nice to know."

There was no time for damage control. Courtney took a breath and tried again. "Anyway, back to my... problem," she said, wrapping her tongue around the del-icate euphemism. "I don't want to have to deal with phonies, wondering if that love light I see in their eyes is meant for me or my bank account. And I don't have the time to search for that one honest man my father seems to think I can find. This way, we both get something we want. I get my inheritance and you get a lot more money than you could earn in two years with that hammer."

No matter how she tried to dress it up, she was trying to buy him. Integrity, and his name, just weren't for sale. "I like honest work, Ms. Tamberlaine, and this—"

"There's nothing dishonest about this. Well, maybe from Parsons's point of view, but—"

Another character in her little drama? "Parsons?"

She nodded. "My father's lawyer. He's the one insisting on carrying out the terms of the will to the letter."

At least someone in her world had some integrity. "And how is he going to be satisfied that this marriage you propose is on the level? Is he going to be there on the honeymoon, taking pictures?"

"He'll be there at the wedding, and as for the rest, there isn't going to be a honeymoon, not in the sense you mean. Nor a consummation, either. Parsons is just going to have to take my word for it. And he will." She could play the loving wife. She could be very convincing if she had to.

John pitied Parsons, whoever he was. "Foolish man."

Gabriel didn't seem quite as hardened as before, but she wasn't cheering just yet. "So, do we have a deal, Gabriel?"

Is that the impression he had given her? He shook his head. "We do not. I'm not for sale...or rent, Ms. Tamberlaine."

He saw what he took to be disappointment enter the woman's eyes. None of his affair, he told himself. No matter what she said, she'd probably have someone else lined up before he reached his van. Someone who would jump when she pulled the string. That wasn't him.

John looked down at his daughter. She'd been nursing that last bit of lemonade for a while now. Katie seemed oblivious to what was going on around her. "Finished, Katie?"

Even at four, Katie knew what that tone meant. No more fooling around. She sucked on her straw loudly, then retired it. "Finished."

"Okay, we have to go, honey." John looked at his watch. Maybe it would be better all around if he got an early start in the morning. Way early, before Her Highness was up. He could leave Katie with Adrienne. His neighbor was always more than willing to watch Katie. That way, he could try to catch up to his schedule.

"Thanks for the lemonade, Ms. Tamberlaine." John began to usher Katie toward the rear exit. "I'll be back tomorrow. To work on the guest house," he added pointedly.

Katie broke away from her father and ran back to Courtney. To Courtney's surprise, she tugged her down to her level and wrapped warm, childish arms around her neck.

"I'll talk to him," Katie promised in a hot whisper that grazed Courtney's cheek.

Precocious, that was the word for her, Courtney thought as she rose back to her feet. She watched the duo leave. As for Katie's father, she decided, there were many words that could be used to describe him, the most polite of which was jackass.

Chapter Three

John tugged on the car seat's electric blue strap. The left one always seemed to get so tangled. He pulled it over, inserting the metal tab into the slot with a click, then tested it to satisfy himself that it was secure. It was.

He could tell Katie was trying very hard not to squirm as he buckled her into the car seat. At four, she was both too young and too light to be allowed to sit in the car with only a seat belt holding her in place. He'd explained that to her on a number of occasions and she had taken it all in solemnly, but he knew she didn't like it. She didn't like being restrained. Maybe in a way it reminded her of all those tubes she'd had invading her little body while she'd laid in the hospital bed.

Some people would have said that, at two, she would have been too young to remember, but he knew Katie. She remembered. He'd have taken bets that, somehow, she was able to recall everything from the moment she had first opened her eyes on this world of theirs. Why else would she have seemed so worldly-wise at times?

He patted her arm. "Just another few months and a few more pounds, honey."

Age wasn't the only requirement California set down in its law governing car seats. She had to weigh more than forty pounds. There were times, late at night, when he laid awake and worried if she ever would.

Katie sighed patiently. Sometimes he wondered who the adult was in their relationship. His birth certificate ascribed that right to him, but John certainly felt like a lost kid at times. A lost kid just trying to find his way through an ever-twisting maze of doctors and bills. At twenty, when he'd first met Diane, John had thought that he had all the answers. Now, eleven years later, he had only questions and uncertainties filling the voids inside of him.

But they'd get through it, he thought as he got in behind the wheel of the '78 van he kept coaxing back to life. They always had before. Just Katie and him against the world.

What more could a man ask for?

Starting the van, John listened to it groan in protest. It shuddered twice before it finally had the good grace to turn over. He patted the dashboard for Katie's amusement.

"Good old van," they said together and then laughed. It warmed his heart, taking the bitter taste from his mouth. The one he'd acquired when the Tamberlaine woman had hit him between the eyes with her bizarre proposition.

Marriage. The woman had to be a lunatic. Completely certifiable. Or maybe it really was just an elaborate hoax. No, he reconsidered, whatever else it was, it wasn't a hoax. The look in her eyes when she'd asked had said otherwise. She'd looked serious, uncomfortable. As if she felt her back was to the wall.

Not his problem, he reminded himself. He had enough to deal with on his own without wondering what was on some spoiled, scatterbrained woman's mind. His responsibility to her began and ended with the renovations on her guest house. End of story.

Slowly, John eased the vehicle out of the wide, winding driveway.

"Did you like her?"

He hit the brake the second he saw the car in the rearview mirror. A blazing red Mercedes parked almost squarely in his path. It hadn't been there when he'd arrived this morning. It almost wasn't there now. If he hadn't taken a second look, the car's right fender would have been under his rear wheel.

John curbed the urge to swear and pulled the steering wheel all the way to the right. "Who?"

Katie wiggled her toes. She didn't like sitting in the car seat. It was too much like a baby seat. Like a high chair. But she didn't complain. She knew her daddy only wanted to keep her safe. Daddy was always worried about keeping her safe, telling her not to play too long, not to get too tired. Making her eat that yucky food he said was good for her when all she wanted was ice cream. A whole big pile of ice cream. Cherry.

She bet if that lady were her mommy, she'd let her eat all the cherry ice cream she wanted. "The lady who looks like Mommy."

John exhaled as he eased his vehicle past the crookedly parked car. There was a hairbreadth of space between them. He wondered if the Mercedes belonged to the Tamberlaine woman. It seemed like her style. Vivid, in-your-face. Just like her. Parked almost sideways was just about the way he'd expect her to leave her car. With complete disregard for everyone else. People like that really annoyed the hell out of him.

He glanced at his daughter. Katie had that puckered look on her face, the one she wore when she was concentrating on something with all her might, unwilling to let it go just yet.

Just like the way she had hung on to life when she was first born. The doctors hadn't thought she'd make it through the night. She'd proved them all wrong and made it through not one night but more than fifteen hundred nights since then.

His face softened when he looked at her, even though the topic didn't please him. "I don't know her well enough to like her."

That wasn't strictly true. John felt he knew enough to *dis*like Courtney Tamberlaine, but he didn't say as much to Katie. If she found it in that big heart of hers to like the woman, he wasn't going to say anything against her.

Katie raised her sharp little chin. "Well, I liked her." She slanted a look at her father. "She hugs nice."

John almost laughed out loud, not at what Katie said, but at the way she looked when she said it. Damn, if she wasn't trying to manipulate him. Four, going on forty, with feminine wiles just aching to burst out. He pitied the man who was going to try to win her. Pity him? Hell, he'd probably cut the first guy who tried to come near his daughter off at the knees at the least sign of interest, he decided. No sweaty, hormonal kid was going to put the moves on *his* little girl and live.

There was a light at the end of the street. As they reached it, it turned a bright red.

"*You* hug nice," he corrected. "She just reacted."

John leaned over, bringing his face close to hers. "Who's the world's best hugger?"

Katie beamed at the familiar question and jerked a thumb at her chest. "I am."

"You bet your little bottom you are." John saw the look in her eyes, the one, even at her tender age, he knew she was trying to hide. He felt his heart twist within his chest. She was exhausted and she didn't want him to know. "Tired, honey?"

Katie moved her shoulders in a half shrug. There was no use in fibbing. Daddy could always tell if she was. "A little."

"We'll be home soon," he promised.

The light was just barely turning green again before he was pressing down on the accelerator. Guilt pricked at him. It was a good thing he'd left when he had. He'd kept Katie out too long as it was, he upbraided himself. Selfish, selfish.

He hadn't been thinking of her when he'd brought Katie along with him today, but of himself. Just because he wanted her near him, to absorb as much as he could of her joy and her innocence, storing it in his memory against the day that—

No, damn it. He wasn't going to get maudlin. Katie was going to be fine and live long enough to make him a great-grandfather several times over.

Provided he ever let a guy near her, of course.

Hands tightening impatiently on the wheel as he stopped at another red light, John looked at his daughter again. Katie was leaning against the black upholstery. She looked so small, so frail.

Dynamite sticks were small, too, he insisted silently. She was going to be just great. There was no point in worrying, it didn't accomplish anything.

But he did, anyway. Especially in the wee hours of the night, when worry ate away at him like a persistent, relentless shrew, until it threatened to leave nothing of him at all.

And worry had fertile ground. There was almost no money left in his bank account. He couldn't work at a regular job because he had to take so much time off to be with Katie when she was sick—that meant no health insurance. Private plans wouldn't take her. Even if they did, the payments would have been prohibitive.

His mouth curved in a smile with no humor. And that Tamberlaine woman thought *her* back was to the wall. She had nothing on him.

By the time John pulled up in the driveway of the tidy, daisy-bordered three-bedroom house where he and Katie lived, Katie had fallen asleep. It wasn't that long a trip from the Tamberlaine estate to his home, but Katie had suddenly become very tired.

It hit that way, John thought bitterly, getting out. Coming unannounced, sapping all the energy that ran through her veins, energy that should have been hers to use as she pleased.

Opening the passenger door, John hesitated a moment, watching Katie sleep. Had there *ever* been anything created as perfect as his little girl?

He doubted it.

John touched her cheek lightly. She stirred a little, holding on to sleep as if it were a blanket covering her. "We're home, Tiger," he whispered.

The small dark lashes that crested the swell of her cheeks fluttered open. She was still drowsy as she rubbed her eyes. "I'm not asleep."

"Of course you're not." Unstrapping her, he lifted

Katie out of the seat. Rather than put her down on the ground, he cradled her against him and turned toward the house.

This time, Katie did squirm just a little. He could tell just how tired she was by the effort she made. "I can walk, Daddy."

He unlocked the front door, then shut it with his elbow. "I know that. I just like carrying you." He grinned down into her open face as he walked down the hall to the rear of the house. "This way you go where I say."

A lower lip stuck out petulantly. "To bed?"

He nodded, crossing the threshold into her room. Like Katie, it glowed of sunshine. With one hand, he pulled back the covers on her bed. Matching the curtains, they were her favorite color. Pink.

"Just for a nap."

She locked her hands around his neck as he eased her down onto the bed. "But I'm not tired."

"Maybe, but I am. Humor me." He looked around for Mr. Softy, her once plush, once white rabbit. The droopy-eared stuffed animal was sitting on the window seat, listing to one side where his cotton batting had shifted. "You want to make your old dad happy, don't you?"

Katie propped herself up on one elbow, even though it made her more tired. "Can't I make you happy some other way?"

"Nope." He plucked the rabbit from the window seat and brought it over to Katie. Picking up her arm, he tucked it around the treasured rabbit. It was the one thing that Diane had given Katie before leaving. Maybe that was why she loved the ragged toy so much.

Katie sighed mightily, resigned to her fate. Even now,

her eyes were closing. "Okay, but can *you* make *me* happy?"

He sat down on the edge of the juvenile bed he had built for her with his own hands. They had stenciled in the design on the headboard together, which might have explained why it was so crooked, John thought fondly.

He brushed the wispy bangs away from her eyes. "I try."

She curled into Mr. Softy. "Can I go with you to see the lady when you go back to work?"

He didn't think that was a very good idea. For either of them. "Katie, I—"

"Please?"

She held his soul in those eyes of hers, he thought. When she looked at him like that, he could deny her absolutely nothing. John shook his head, surrendering.

"Someday, I'm going to learn how to say no to you. Okay, but you have to stay out of her way." *We both do,* he added silently.

Katie was the soul of solemnity. "I promise."

Rising, John tucked the sheet around her. Katie's eyes had fluttered shut again, despite her protests.

For a moment, John just stood there, watching her sleep. God, what would he ever do without her? Blowing out a deep, long breath, he eased himself slowly from the room.

He went straight to the telephone in the kitchen. Picking up the receiver, he tapped the first button on his automatic dialer. Katie's heart specialist.

As he heard the combination of tones play in the receiver, he could feel his own heart sink within him. A four-year-old shouldn't have a heart specialist, he thought bitterly. All she should have is a pediatrician, and routine innoculations, not electrocardiograms.

It wasn't fair.

It could have been worse, he reminded himself as he listened to the phone ringing on the other end. He above all people knew just how much worse it could really be.

So now what, Courtney thought, hating this helpless feeling dancing through her. Now what did she do?

Restless, she paced about her bedroom, moving around in large concentric circles.

Just like her life right now, she thought, frustrated.

Mandy had had a party to go to. She had driven off in her red Mercedes just a few minutes ago after trying unsuccessfully to talk her into coming along.

But Courtney wasn't in the mood for parties. After trying to ignore reality for so long, it had finally sunk in, announcing itself with sharp claws that stung as they scratched along her consciousness.

If she didn't abide by her father's ironclad wishes, Courtney was going to have to give up a life she'd come to take for granted. And by doing so, become something other than who she was.

Kicking aside a pair of shoes in her path, she stopped at the edge of the long, honey-colored bureau. A rectangular mirror, as long as the oversized bureau, hung directly behind it, bounced her image back at her. She looked worried.

She *was* worried.

There was a single, silver-framed photograph standing on her bureau. She drew the frame to her. Her eyes blurred a little as they washed over her father's picture. He'd been a silver-haired, strikingly handsome man with kind eyes and a mouth that was perpetually curved in a warm smile, even to the very end.

Eleven years and she still missed him. Missed the

sound of his voice, his booming laugh that filled up all the corners of the house.

Lovingly, she ran her fingers along the frame, then feathered them lightly down the image trapped beneath the glass.

What was going to happen now?

"I don't know how to be anyone else but me, Daddy. You're not around anymore to bully me and tell me to do the right thing." She sighed, setting the frame down again. "Although I do try." She pressed her lips together. "But it's hard, without you around."

Not that the woman she had become could be thought of as a failure in any sense of the word. Following in her father's footsteps, she had chaired several local charities and the national one he had founded, giving far more of herself than anyone suspected.

That didn't, however, qualify her for any sort of gainful employment. She was well aware of that. If she became forced to supplement her income with some sort of a career, she had absolutely no idea what she was qualified to do.

She ran a tentative fingertip along the edge of the frame. "In case you hadn't noticed, there aren't many openings in the want ads for formerly well-to-do heiresses."

Want ads. She thought of what Mandy had laughingly suggested—advertising for a husband. She was beginning to think that would be the only way she'd find the kind of man who would fit her father's requirements, especially in the time she had left.

But any man who *did* fit her father's idea of a good, solid man would have to be trained if he was to fit into her way of life.

Certainly that lamebrained, muscle-bound laborer

would have had to have been instructed—probably on how to do everything but walk. That, she recalled, momentarily letting her mind drift, he did very well. Sleek, economized movements, like a cat. No, like a panther.

A panther with a tool belt.

Had her father really expected her to marry someone like that? And be happy? How could she? She and someone like that man had nothing in common outside of both being human and living in Southern California.

And to think, she had all but thrown herself at him. Well, not *herself,* she amended, but her wallet. Still, he had deliberately insulted her by not "catching."

Maybe, in some perverse way, he'd thought he was too good for her. College graduate, ha! If he was a college graduate, then she was Mother Teresa. He'd probably said that just to annoy her.

And he'd succeeded.

Thank goodness he hadn't taken her up on her hasty offer. Then she'd really be stuck.

Instead of what she was now.

Stuck.

Courtney flounced down on her king-sized bed, feeling absolutely hopeless. She hadn't felt remotely close to this sort of helplessness since her father had died. Then she'd felt that way because she couldn't alter what had happened, couldn't barter with God for five more minutes with the one person she loved more than anyone. Helplessness had all but destroyed her then.

Now it just confused her.

So now what? Courtney wondered again.

A stubborn resolve not to be defeated rose above the layers of despair, fighting its way to the surface. Determined, Courtney pulled the telephone from her nightstand.

Courtney was going to *make* Parsons listen to reason. The right man didn't just pop up like bread from a toaster slot. If he did, all marriages would be fairy tales. Instead of what they were. None of the marriages she knew had lasted more than a few years.

Even royalty didn't seem to have the knack anymore. How *was* she expected to find the right man in less than a month?

Never mind that she'd had the past eleven years to get down to business. Now that she was looking at the matter seriously, she realized she needed more time to give it her best shot. Surely, Parsons would understand that.

Parsons, as it turned out, had a heart made out of stone. Granite.

Just like that Gage's muscles. Gabriel's, she corrected herself.

Gabriel.

Like the archangel. Only there wasn't anything angelic about the man. Except, maybe for his face...

She was letting her mind stray, she upbraided herself. And right now, she couldn't afford that. Having connected to Parsons's office, she'd made her plea and was being railroaded. As Parsons droned on in a monotone, she opened her mouth to launch another eloquent argument. Just then the annoying beep of a call trying to get through sounded. She ignored it.

Courtney rocked forward, holding on to the receiver with both hands. "Mr. Parsons, I will not be bullied. I—"

The infernal beeping came again. That was the third time someone had called and hung up, only to try again in less than five minutes. Obviously, ignoring the annoying noise wasn't going to make whoever was calling go away.

"Hold on, will you?" she asked impatiently. "There's someone on the other line and they obviously don't know when to take no for an answer."

"Seems to be a great deal of that going ar—"

Courtney hit the hold button. It gave her heart a slight boost to cut Parsons off before he could finish.

"Yes?" she snapped.

Hang up. Now, while you still have the chance. John's emotions warred with his fatalistic sense of what had to be. "Ms. Tamberlaine?"

The deep voice sounded vaguely familiar, but Courtney couldn't place it. "Yes, who is this?"

An idiot. He was going to regret this, John thought. But there was no other way out for him. For them. He wasn't doing this for himself, but for Katie. And for Katie, he'd walk through fire.

"This is John Gabriel, Ms. Tamberlaine." He had to push the rest of the words out. "Is there somewhere we can meet to talk about that offer you made earlier today?"

Pleasure, rimmed with the oddest sting of disappointment, ribboned through her. Somehow, she'd actually believed him when he'd said that he couldn't be bought. She'd believed that he was different.

Deep down she should have realized that once you scratched the surface, people were all alike. They just had different price tags. How many times had she been taught that lesson? There was no reason to feel like a child who'd come down on Christmas morning to discover that Santa Claus was really just a myth.

"Hold on a minute," she said crisply. "I have to get rid of another call."

Yes, John thought, he was going to really regret this. But Katie meant far more to him than his pride and was worth anything he had to endure.

And something told him that he had just opened himself up to endure a great deal.

Chapter Four

It shouldn't be this way.

Courtney searched the rarely used well-stocked bar that her father had flown in from Japan more than twenty years ago. Where the hell was the bottle of tonic? She felt as if she were walking in slow motion through someone else's dream. It certainly wasn't her dream.

She glanced back at the good-looking man sitting on her pristine white, oversize sofa. His presence almost dwarfed it. It wasn't so much that he was such a big man as that he somehow seemed larger than life. Larger than her life.

But even though he was gorgeous in a raw, earthy sort of way that cut clear down to the bone, that didn't change anything. Didn't change what she was feeling about this discussion they were about to have.

Emotions collided within her like so many marbles

being tossed around in an upended box. She felt sad, angry, rebellious. And trapped.

This certainly wasn't the way she'd once envisioned feeling about her groom-to-be. Or about her wedding-to-be. She should be euphoric, overjoyed, giddy. And head over heels in love, or at least some reasonable facsimile thereof.

Not pragmatic.

But that was the word that best described her feelings as she faced the ceremony that lay ahead of her. Pragmatic.

Courtney placed a chunky multifaceted glass on the ornate bar. This was probably the way a princess might have felt two hundred years ago when her father gave her hand in marriage to some ogre of a black prince just to extend the borders of the realm, or to ensure peace. Not quite human, a pawn to some higher purpose.

Nothing so lofty was going on now, of course, she thought, finally finding the elusive tonic amid the cluster of barely touched bottles of alcohol. It had been right in front of her all along.

Muttering, she poured the clear liquid over the ice and gin already in the glass.

This is all your fault, Daddy. If you'd have let me go about this in my own way, I would have found a good man. Eventually. If one is to be found. And if I didn't, well, I would have enjoyed the hunt. But not this. This is negotiating across a bargaining table. This is business. Marriage isn't supposed to be business.

Courtney stared moodily at the back of Gabriel's head as she returned with the drink he'd requested once she had prodded him. He turned just then and she dropped her eyes before she thought better of it. When she raised them again and met his gaze, her own was defiant.

"Your gin and tonic."

Courtney handed him his drink and sat down across from him. Subconsciously, she was using the distance to mark an invisible line between them. This wasn't going to be a friendly discussion and they both knew it.

"Thanks." But rather than take a sip, he held the glass in both hands.

Mandy's poodle, Cuddles, hopped onto the love seat beside her, yapped and then jumped off to explore the room again. The dog was a bundle of nerves tonight.

That made two of them.

What was it about this man that made her feel so awkward, so clumsy? Was it because she felt he was sitting in judgment of her, looking into her soul with those deep, liquid green eyes of his? Hell, she didn't care what he thought. What anyone thought. She'd thumbed her nose at other people's opinions all her life.

And she'd thumb her nose at his. Once the bargain was sealed.

Why wasn't he saying something? Was he going to stare at her like that all evening? He was the one who had called her this afternoon, not the other way around.

Tucking her legs beneath her, she shifted on the love seat. "So where is Katie?"

She was all legs, he thought. His eyes drifted slowly along the long, sleek lines as she moved her legs under her. Her shorts rode up and she tugged on the hem to get them back into place. The white shorts could hardly be called decent.

But then, neither could she. Not with the offer she had made him.

He needed the offer, but that didn't mean he didn't resent her for making it. Or himself for taking it. Things shouldn't be done this way. Even when he had married

Diane, there was the illusion of a happy life ahead of them. Here, there was nothing.

Just business.

That made it simpler. And more complicated.

"Home." He cradled the glass between his hands, looking down at the shimmering liquid. "With a sitter." He raised his eyes to Courtney's face. "I didn't think she should be listening to this."

Why? Don't you want her to see Daddy sell out?

The thought flashed across her mind and she almost said the words out loud. She caught herself just in time. Courtney knew she was at cross-purposes with herself, but she couldn't help feeling just a shade bitter about all this.

She felt no triumph at having been right all along. She'd said everyone could be bought, and they could. Gabriel was no different, with his aloof bearing and his shoulders out to here. He was just like all the others. The amount she'd quoted to him had apparently just taken longer for him to process. Now that it had finally sunk in, he was here, ready to sign on the dotted line.

"No," she agreed. "I don't suppose she should." Suddenly needing something to hold on to, Courtney picked up one of the azure-fringed suede throw pillows she had scattered along both pieces of furniture and hugged it to her. "Four is very young to lose your illusions."

Something in Courtney's voice caught his attention, arousing his curiosity. "How old were you when you lost yours?"

She shrugged, toying with the edge of the pillow. "I don't remember. It was a gradual thing, not like finding out there was no Santa Claus." Her father had said that she was born old. And jaded. Maybe she had been. And the men she'd met had only helped her along the rest of the way. "No crash of thunder." Her eyes shifted to his face. "As a matter of fact, you might say that it's still an ongoing process."

There was an accusing look in her eyes. But that was ridiculous. He hadn't done anything to her. It was himself he had hurt. He'd sold out his principles. But none of that had anything to do with her.

Just him.

And Katie.

Courtney studied Gabriel's face as he sat there in silence. He was relating to her, or at least commiserating. She could see it. "How old were you?"

John shrugged, surprised that she would want to know anything personal about him.

"I can't remember, either." He paused, thinking. "I don't think I ever had any."

An image of Diane rose in his mind and he remembered how good it had felt in the beginning. To finally love someone. To finally have things feel as if they were coming together.

But then they had only fallen apart again.

"Well, maybe for a while," he allowed, "but then I grew up."

A sad smile she didn't seem fully conscious of played on her lips. It wasn't the sarcastic one he'd seen before. In a way, it almost made her seem soft, he thought. More than soft, vulnerable. Probably just a ploy.

Suddenly feeling as if he needed it, John took a long sip of his drink. His eyes watered instantly and it was all he could do to keep from coughing and spitting it out. His throat felt raw. The drink was almost pure gin. He couldn't help wondering if she'd done that on purpose.

Taking a deep breath to regain his composure, he set the glass down on the massive coffee table that separated them.

Courtney seemed oblivious to his dilemma. "Yes, I guess that's the word for it. Growing up."

"That's two words," he said mildly, pointing out the obvious.

"Whatever." She didn't like being corrected. Courtney turned her eyes up to his. "Well, no point in dwelling on things that can't be. We need to be moving on with things that have to be, right?" She didn't wait for a response. "I take it you've come to discuss the fine points of this..." She paused, searching for a euphemism she could live with. "Um, 'merger.'" As good as any, she supposed. "Am I right?"

He didn't answer immediately. They were talking about it, but he just couldn't believe he was actually considering this "marriage of convenience" she had proposed. If he had any sense left, he'd get up and run, not walk, to the front door and put this—and her—behind him as fast as humanly possible.

But then he thought of what the doctor had said when he'd called today after Katie had fallen asleep. According to the results of the latest battery of tests the hospital had performed, Katie needed the operation to repair the hole in her heart sooner than he'd anticipated.

And a lot sooner than his bank account had anticipated.

There was already a second mortgage on the house thanks to the result of paying off the last surgery. There was no way in God's green earth he could get another loan.

The only other alternative he had left to him was to turn to Diane's parents and hope that some miracle had occurred to turn them into human beings instead of the bloodless hypocrites they were.

He'd rather crawl on his belly through the desert than ask Howard and Elizabeth Divers for anything. They had made it quite clear what they thought of him. They regarded Katie not as their granddaughter but as his child. He'd made the mistake of approaching them with condolences at Diane's funeral. He had gotten verbal abuse in return. They had nothing but their hate to sustain them in the autumn of their years. So be it.

It was better to turn to a stranger, even if it meant striking up a deal with the devil.

In a way, he supposed, he was earning the money. Picking up the drink again, he took another sip. It went down smoother this time, now that he knew what to expect. He wondered if the same would be true of Courtney. "You said two hundred thousand dollars."

He certainly didn't waste any time. Well, what did she expect? She already knew that Gabriel didn't have the finesse of some of the charming roués she'd known in her time. The ones who had silver tongues and made the mistake of thinking she was simple enough to be talked out of her money.

They'd learned. And so would he if he had any thoughts of getting more.

The smile on her lips was steely. "Ah, the finest point of all in your estimation, I'd wager." Her eyes narrowed. *Was* he going to try to get her to agree to more? "Before we go any further, I want you to know that my offer is nonnegotiable."

Damn, if it wasn't for Katie, he'd tell her where she could put that money, dollar by dollar... He wasn't trying to cheat her out of her money—she was the one who had made the offer, and set the price.

Somehow, he maintained an impassive expression. "Two hundred thousand will be fine."

The surrender surprised her. In actuality, she'd been prepared to go higher if need be. Courtney studied him, looking beyond the tight, firm muscles and the chiseled planes of his face, and far beyond the curling dark blond hair that whispered along his wide shoulders.

He was playing it safe. She would have thought that Gabriel was a risk taker. He had the bearing of someone who would try to outrace the wind for the sheer thrill of it.

Wrong again, she mused.

Courtney tossed aside the pillow and moved forward on the love seat. "Good."

He wondered if she'd worn that blouse on purpose. Hot pink and tied just beneath her breasts, the jaunty knot strategically drew his eyes to the tempting hint of cleavage that was peering out. It gave a man pause and messed with his head.

Which made her offer even harder to understand. Why would such an attractive woman have to resort to paying a stranger two hundred thousand dollars to marry her? He knew of half a dozen places where she could walk in and just crook her finger. Five or more ready and willing men would be at her side before the motion was completed.

"There is, however," he told her, "one more thing I do want."

She arched a brow. Here it came. Demands. Courtney straightened her shoulders, a soldier waiting for the first volley from the enemy. She dropped her voice down to a steely whisper, despite the artificial smile on her face. "And that is?"

John didn't bother pretending to return her smile.

"That you change your tone when you talk to me. Especially around Katie."

Courtney inclined her head. "Don't worry, Gabriel. I won't make her feel as if her father compromised himself."

That was harsh, and she knew it. Courtney bit her lip, waiting for his reaction. She saw something dark and dangerous move across his face, as if he were struggling to hold on to his temper.

He didn't like her, Courtney realized. In a way, though she'd gone out of her way to bait him, that bothered her. She didn't like being disliked. But he liked her money, and in the end, that was all that mattered.

She laughed softly to herself. It was almost a given—in the end, every man always liked her money better than her.

Maybe she was being perverse tonight, or maybe it was to pay him back for disappointing her and turning out to be just another man with no integrity. Whatever the reason, she pushed the envelope a little further.

"By the way, why did you? Compromise yourself, that is. You sounded so lofty earlier, about people not being bought." Her eyes narrowed, pinning him. "Was it because you didn't believe I was serious, or because you were hoping I'd come back with a better offer?"

He was reminded of a scene from a classic movie, of Jimmy Cagney shoving a grapefruit into his girlfriend's face because she'd gotten on his nerves. John knew exactly how old Jimmy's character must have felt a second before he gave in to his impulse.

His fingers tightened around the widemouthed glass in his hands. Why he was doing it was his business, and would remain that way. If she thought he was some deadbeat, well, that was her mistake. He didn't much care what she thought of him or his motives, as long as she kept her opinion to herself when she was around Katie.

"A better offer than living with you?" His mouth curved sardonically. "I didn't think there could be a better offer than that, Ms. Tamberlaine."

Alarms went off inside her head, but she quelled them. Nothing here she couldn't handle, she told herself. "Under the circumstances, maybe you'd better call me Courtney."

"Fine." He raised his glass, toasting her. "Courtney."

Her name came out in a purr that stirred something within her. Something deep and recessed. The alarms multiplied ten-fold.

"Let's get one thing straight, Gabriel. This is strictly a business arrangement. There are ground rules. You help me and I'll pay you for your 'trouble.' You and your daughter will live here after the wedding, but you'll have your own room and, for the most part, your own life—as long as that life doesn't embarrass me," she added pointedly.

It amazed him just how tightly he could hold on to his temper when it involved Katie. "I'll try my best not to scratch in public."

"Oh, it goes far beyond scratching, Gabriel. You can see whomever you want in private, but..." Her voice trailed off for a second as she looked for a way to put this that would get through to him. "Do you understand the word 'discreet'?"

His expression darkened a degree as his eyes held hers. "Do you understand the word 'insulting'?"

She raised both hands in mock surrender. "Sorry, I forgot. You're a college graduate."

He'd had pretty much enough of this game she was playing. "And you are insufferable."

Well, at least he was honest. And maybe she'd asked for it. "You don't have to like me, Gabriel. You just have to marry me." She held up two fingers. "Two years, two hundred thousand dollars. The first installment, fifty thousand dollars, will be placed in your bank account the day we get married. I assume you have one."

"I have one," he replied tersely.

That was it, he thought. The bottom line. He was selling his soul for two hundred thousand dollars.

No, for Katie. He had to remember that. He was doing this for Katie. For the one bright spot in his universe. "And after two years?"

She recited it as if it were going to happen to someone else. The only way she had a prayer of getting through this was by keeping it all at a distance. "Two years is the requirement stated in the will. After that, we wait a decent interval, then get a divorce and you go your own way, a lot richer than you've ever dreamed."

His eyes darkened. "You don't know a damn thing about my dreams, lady."

Had she been standing, Courtney would have taken a step back. She could almost touch his anger.

Catching hold of his temper, John contemplated his glass philosophically. "Wow, married and divorced and I haven't even finished my drink, yet. The nineties just take your breath away, don't they?"

The glimpse into his darker side had left her momentarily numbed. Emerging, she rallied. "That sarcasm clause you tossed my way earlier? The one about not having a sarcastic tone when I address you?" John raised a brow, waiting for her to continue. "Well, it goes both ways. I don't want to hear it, either. When we're around my friends, and especially my lawyer, I want you to act the loving husband."

That was going to be a stretch. Humor twisted his mouth. "In your case, I take that to mean refraining from strangling you."

He was a cocky one. Still, there was something about his smile that got to her. "Right. You can't strangle me and I can't shoot you."

For a moment, he almost liked her. Almost. John laughed, finishing his drink. Leaving the glass on the table, he put out his hand to her. "Deal."

Sliding her legs out from beneath her, Courtney moved forward on the love seat and placed her hand in his. His grip was strong, firm. His hand seemed to swallow hers up.

"Deal," she repeated. She slipped her hand from his. The warmth remained with her. "Now, about Katie."

If there had been an open window for a moment, it was shut again. "Let me worry about Katie."

What did he think she was going to do, sell her into slavery? She liked the little girl. A hell of a lot more than she liked him.

Courtney ignored his protest. "As she will be my stepdaughter, I should take an interest in her. There are private preschools that—"

"Stick to your poodles."

There was no mistaking his tone. It vaguely reminded her of her father's, one of the few times he'd lost his temper with her. Courtney bristled. "I don't have poodles." She waved at the ball of white fluff in the corner. Cuddles was asleep. "The dog is Mandy's. I'm just letting it stay here until she comes in for a landing."

It wasn't the first time Mandy had left Cuddles with

her. Courtney rather liked the little dog with its quick pink tongue. At least it was honest in its affection. It didn't have to be bought.

"Mandy," John repeated. "Your sister?" There was a hell of a lot of things he didn't know about the woman he was binding himself to for two years. How many lovers had she had?

It shouldn't have been the first question that occurred to him, but it was. He dismissed it. That was her business and not his. He wouldn't have asked it of a member of a firm he was joining and he shouldn't be wondering about it now.

"My friend," she corrected. He was going to have to know that if he was going to be her husband. As the litany of things she was going to have to teach him multiplied in her mind, her head began to ache.

He thought a moment, then nodded, making the logical conclusion. "The petite brunette I saw earlier with her nose pressed against the French doors?"

It was an apt description. "The very same. She'll be my maid of honor since she suggested you." Mandy was going to love this, Courtney thought. Her eyes shifted to John. "Would Katie like to be the flower girl?"

Her thoughtfulness toward his daughter surprised him. But she was probably just doing it to please some fantasy she was creating for herself. No sense in giving the woman points where none were due. "Is this going to be a three-ring circus?"

This was her wedding, she'd have as many rings as she damn well pleased. After all, she was paying for it.

She held up her index finger. "One ring. It would look strange if I didn't invite some people." She might as well think of it as a party, Courtney resigned herself.

He'd rather have as few people witnessing this as possible. "Maybe they'll just think you were overcome with love."

"Maybe." Actually, it would be something that several of her friends would probably believe, once they saw Gabriel. "How soon can you make yourself available?" He looked at her oddly. "For the wedding," she added, stifling an unexpected flutter in the pit of her stomach.

His schedule book was painfully blank. "Right now, yours is the only job I have." He shrugged ruefully. "It's been a dry season for renovations."

For a moment, she wondered what that had to feel like, worrying about where your next paycheck was coming from. It had to be horrible.

"Well, it works out because, as of right now, you're not going to be doing any more carpentry." She saw rebellion in his eyes. It looked as if every step was going to have to be negotiated. "It wouldn't look right."

He balked at having her dictate to him, at having *anyone* dictate to him, but he had signed on for this and he was going to have to make the best of it. He shrugged indifferently. "You're paying the tab."

"Yes," she said, her eyes on his. "I am."

This was exactly what she wanted, what she needed. Her prayers were answered. So why the hell did she resent him for doing exactly what she wanted him to do? For selling himself out to her? Why did she feel as if she'd just been cheated of something?

She wasn't being cheated of anything, she insisted fiercely. She was being assured of her inheritance.

Courtney pushed ahead. "All right. We can get married in twelve days. That still gives us plenty of time to beat the deadline by a good two weeks. And enough time to get a prenuptial agreement signed."

He couldn't help grinning. It was all so ludicrous. Any second now, he was going to wake up to discover it was all a bad dream. That Katie was a normal, healthy four-year-old and Courtney Tamberlaine was just a figment of his overactive imagination.

"Prenuptial agreement," he echoed. "Do I get to draw up one, too?"

His words, or maybe his grin, coaxed one in kind from her. "Don't worry, you haven't got anything I want."

He glanced toward the door, but it was closed. "That wouldn't sound very romantic if anyone happened to be eavesdropping."

Courtney let out a sigh. "Along with not having illusions, I stopped being a romantic a long, long time ago."

And it bothered her, he thought. She was acting as if it didn't, but the look in her eyes told him differently. "Then we've got something in common." His eyes held hers. "Pity, isn't it?"

She had no idea what to say to that, but something sad and distant within her agreed with him.

Chapter Five

"So you do like her, right, Daddy? I told you you would."

John could see his daughter's reflection in the bottom right-hand corner of the beveled mirror. Katie was almost jumping up and down with glee. If she wasn't careful, he thought with a smile, she was going to use up all the oxygen within the tiny room the priest had brought them to.

Giving the striped tie he'd just put on one final adjustment, John turned and looked down at his daughter. Her enthusiasm was radiating from every single pore.

He wished it was contagious.

Aware of his scrutiny, Katie carefully smoothed down her dress, primping for his benefit. She was wearing her first long dress, an icy blue frock that almost looked white in the right light. It just whispered along her new white patent leather shoes.

She looked like an angel, he thought.

Courtney had selected the dress for her, as she had all the clothes for this little play. She'd taken care of all the details, proving to be a veritable whirlwind of activity. He really hadn't thought she could pull it off. But, to his amazement, everything seemed to be dovetailing now. He had to hand it to her, Courtney was good at organizing and manipulating things.

Just how good, he figured he was going to find out in the months ahead.

John moved his shoulders restlessly beneath his jacket. Though the tuxedo fit as if it were made for him, he still felt constricted. He could move his arms and legs well enough, but that didn't negate the trapped feeling wafting through every part of his body.

He couldn't think of himself right now, he had to think of Katie. She was all that mattered.

John crouched down to her level. Her blue eyes were fairly dancing with excitement. She'd been like this ever since he'd worked up the courage to tell her that he was marrying Courtney.

It was a double-edged sword. While watching her anticipation warmed his heart, it saddened it, too.

Katie was the victim in this, he thought. He and Courtney were entering into this business deal with their eyes opened wide and with no illusions, but it was Katie who stood to get hurt. Katie who believed that this was real. More than anything, he wanted to shield her, to keep her from being bitterly disappointed.

How did you tell a child that you were entering a sham? That the only reason you were even considering it was to get enough money for an operation that would make her well again? Once the operation was performed, she would grow up to be like other children. Katie would run and play and be tapped into an endless source of energy, instead of becoming tired so often.

And then maybe, eventually, she would understand why he had done this.

But he couldn't tell her that now. It was far too much to put on her shoulders. He knew that if he told Katie he was doing this for her, that there was no love between Courtney and him, Katie would feel guilty about his sacrifice.

Far older than her years, Katie understood things like that.

"Well, don't you like her?"

She was waiting for his answer. Waiting for him to admit that she'd been right. John took her hands in his. He couldn't bring himself to lie to her. There seemed to be no right way to do this. "Honey, I want you to remember that no matter what happens, nothing is going to change for us."

Her eyes were laughing at him, as if she thought he was being funny for her benefit. "Yes, it is. I'm getting a mommy."

He could see it happening already. There was that look in her eyes. The look that told him Katie was falling in love with Courtney. There was a lot of love in that fragile little heart. He hated that it was being misdirected under false pretenses. Pretenses he was helping to foster.

Courtney was liable to run right over Katie without even knowing it.

Uncertainty returned to gnaw at him. Not for the first time he contemplated just grabbing Katie's hand and making a run for it. But there was nowhere to run.

And it wouldn't solve his major problem. It wouldn't give him the money for Katie's operation.

Maybe, if he was very careful and kept Katie out of

Courtney's way, the ultimate effect this would have on her would be minimal.

Or maybe Courtney would find it in her heart not to inadvertently hurt Katie too much.

How could Katie *not* be hurt? She thought she was getting a mother, not a business arrangement. There was no way she could come out of this untouched.

"Honey—" he began again, then stopped.

What could he say to her? Katie was only four, an older four than most, but still four. She didn't understand about bills and desperation.

There was a knock on the door. Hearing it, he felt as if he'd just gotten an eleventh-hour reprieve from the governor.

"You decent, Johnny?"

John recognized Mandy's voice. He rose just as the door opened. She didn't bother waiting for him to answer.

"Ready or not, here I come. Two minutes to show time," Mandy announced, then stopped dead as she got her first look at him in a tuxedo. She stared unabashedly. "My, oh, my, but some women do have all the luck."

With a grin, she looked up into his eyes. "We always called Court the lucky one when we were kids." She glanced down at the exuberant child, explaining. "Courtney could fall into a pile of dirt and come up clean, with a diamond in her hand." Mandy slanted another look at John, then exhaled wistfully. Her dress, an adult version of Katie's, rustled as she moved closer to him. "Are there any more like you hanging around the woodpile?"

Though he'd met her only twice now, John had taken a liking to Courtney's best friend and her quirky sense of humor. "I don't know, you'll have to see."

"Daddy's one of a kind," Katie informed her proudly, repeating something she'd heard.

"I can believe that." Circling him, Mandy feathered her hand along the back of his jacket, brushing off an imaginary hair. If his shoulders were any broader, they could have been declared a road.

John heard her sigh behind him. Their eyes met in the mirror.

Mandy's smile widened. "You and I have a date, Johnny. Two years from today, at noon. Church steps. If Court's crazy enough to throw you away then, I get first dibs." Reaching up, she placed her hands on his shoulders and turned him around to face her. "Promise?"

Maybe it was the bottled water they drank. Whatever the cause, the women in this zip code were all crazy, he thought. But at least Mandy was entertaining. Courtney was something else again. Just what he wasn't sure.

He laughed, gently removing her hands. "Sorry, but I'll be out of the game by then."

"Too bad." Mandy sighed again, this time for effect. "Although if I know Court, she'll come to her senses and hang on to you." *What woman wouldn't?* She allowed herself one last, longing look. "Her daddy sure knew what he was doing."

Mandy turned her attention to Katie. She had come here for a reason. "C'mon, Katie, you have to throw flower petals around so your new stepmom can walk on them." She took Katie's hand in hers, then looked over her shoulder at John. "As for you, the priest wants to see you at the altar, pronto. Dead center."

Dead was the word for it, he thought as the door closed again. The click the lock made as it slipped into the groove sounded like the first nail being hammered into his coffin.

Two years. By the time this afternoon was over, he was going to sign away two years of his life.

Two years were going to seem like forever.

He'd thought that nothing could have topped the impression Courtney Tamberlaine created in her bikini.

He'd thought wrong.

She looked incredible now, drifting toward him down the aisle like a fantasy he had conjured up in the small hours of the night when his heart needed comforting. A fantasy that embodied the perfect woman.

He knew she was far from perfect, but she was still a vision. As John Gabriel watched the woman who was to be his wife in name only approach him with slow, rhythmic steps, he thought he had never seen anything so beautiful in his life.

It made him ache for a moment to know that none of this was true.

Having emptied out the contents of her basket in her stroll down the aisle, his daughter was now sitting in the first pew. Beside her, keeping a watchful eye on Katie, was a woman he'd been introduced to as Courtney's Aunt Lisa, who'd flown in just for the occasion.

Katie whispered something to her and the woman smiled, nodding. Katie had made another friend, he thought. It didn't surprise him. She'd probably make friends with everyone here by the time the reception was over. The bride's side of the church was filled with people.

That made the church half-full. His side was conspicuously empty. Though his circle of friends wasn't large, John had deliberately refrained from inviting anyone he knew to this fiasco. He would have passed on having a best man as well, but Courtney had told him that if he didn't have anyone in mind, she would provide someone to stand up for him.

That had galvanized him. The wedding and subsequent marriage might be a sham, but John didn't want one of Courtney's former lovers, or perhaps her present one, standing beside him and sneering while he promised to love and cherish her.

So he'd invited Rick to be his best man. A friend since their first year in college, Rick never passed judgment on anyone and rarely asked questions. It made him the perfect friend as far as John was concerned.

Rick leaned over to him now as Courtney drew closer. "I don't know how the hell you got this lucky, Gabe, or how you managed to keep her a secret from me, but damn, she makes a man's mouth water." Rick only grinned when he saw John's dark eyebrows rise. "Sorry, just had to get that out."

John looked at the approaching woman, nodding at his friend's apology. He could understand Rick's reaction. Courtney was stunning. She would have been stunning if she had elected to walk up the aisle wearing a garment bag.

Beautiful on the outside, empty on the inside, he reminded himself. He'd been on that merry-go-round before. Except this time he knew exactly what he was getting himself into, and why.

He'd known why before, he remembered. Back then, he'd thought he was doing it for love. A love so strong that it hurt him just to breathe.

He was breathing just fine now. In a way, without love to complicate things, the burden was taken off. Maybe it was better this way, after all.

If he worked at it, perhaps he would eventually convince himself.

Without a father or an uncle to pinch-hit, Courtney could have easily marched down the aisle alone. Instead, Courtney had purposely selected Edwin Parsons's arm to be the one she leaned on this day of all days.

When the first strains of the wedding march wafted through the air, Courtney had suppressed a smug smile and taken Parsons's arm. She wanted the man to witness from a front-row seat this charade that she'd been forced to undertake. This way, there would be no room for doubt.

As they began to walk, he still seemed somewhat confused by it all.

She'd come in person to ask him to be the one who escorted her down the aisle. There was no way she was going to miss seeing his expression when he first heard that she was going to fulfill her father's mandate.

She wasn't disappointed.

For once, Parsons's normally dour expression cracked. He'd stared at her, momentarily dumbstruck, as if he couldn't believe that she had finally capitulated. "Then you are going through with this?"

It was evident to her that Parsons thought she was lying in hopes he'd believe her. A lie wouldn't have gotten her anywhere and they both knew it.

"Absolutely." She'd placed a hand over her breast, as if taking a solemn oath. "It was love at first sight. John Gabriel is *everything* Daddy ever wanted for me. I'm only grateful that Daddy found a way to direct me, even after he was gone."

Parsons had looked at her skeptically. Courtney knew she had laid it on a bit thick, but she was enjoying herself.

She wasn't enjoying herself now, she thought. The wedding march echoed in her brain, sounding louder and louder as she drew closer to the altar. Courtney felt as if her knees had suddenly turned to jelly and wouldn't support her. She'd been so sure of herself just a few minutes earlier. Where had this flood of feelings and anxiety come from?

Something within her felt like dying.

She'd lied when she said she'd had no illusions. She did. There was still one illusion left. She'd really thought that when she finally got married, it wouldn't be just a temporary union. That it would be a bonding not just of names spoken by a priest, but of souls.

Next time, she promised herself. Next time it would be real.

And forever.

Moving down the aisle, Courtney nodded toward several people who tried to catch her eye. She made certain that no matter what the condition of her stomach and her knees, her smile remained regal, bright. They'd come for a festive time and she was going to see that they got it.

She saw Katie looking at her. Courtney winked at her and Katie waved. Dimples deepened on both side of her face as she grinned.

The little girl was going to be a knockout when she grew up, Courtney thought. Gabriel had his work cut out for him.

Gabriel. Courtney turned her eyes toward him. Toward the man she'd bought for herself, she thought sarcastically.

The mild contempt she felt faded, and then vanished. Her mouth turned dry. As dry as the desert baking beneath the noonday sun.

She was already aware that he was good-looking—gorgeous, really—but she'd had no idea that he would look this heart stopping in a tuxedo. When she thought about it, she'd assumed that, if anything, Gabriel would look out of place, uncomfortable, in the dark garment. Like a sow's ear instead of a silk purse, to coin a phrase.

But he looked as if he was born to wear a tuxedo. There was an underlying sensuality about him that the finely tailored lines seemed to enhance.

Courtney didn't have to turn to the rear of the church to know that every woman's eyes were firmly riveted on him and not her.

She reached the altar walking on someone else's feet. Somewhere in a haze, she heard the priest ask, "Who gives this woman in holy matrimony?" and was only vaguely aware of Parsons's response.

A light tap on her elbow reminded her to hand Mandy the bouquet she was clutching. She would have gone on holding it just to ground herself to reality.

"Jackpot," Mandy whispered, taking the flowers from her.

Not really, Courtney thought. But maybe, for the benefit of everyone today, if not herself, she could pretend.

"Ready?"

The whispered question ruffled the veil along her cheek. She turned her eyes to John. There was a hint of something, perhaps amusement, in his eyes. At her expense, no doubt.

It served to rally her.

"Geronimo," she whispered back. Not exactly romantic, but it got the message across.

She got through it, even the part about cherishing, without bolting, balking or blowing it. It was only when the priest had pronounced them joined before God and man and urged Gabriel to kiss the bride that she had faltered. When Gabriel leaned into her, she managed to just graze his mouth with her own and then turned instantly to walk down the aisle.

Physical contact, she'd already told him when they'd gone over the prenuptial agreement at Mr. Matthew's office, was to be kept at a minimum. Kissing was at the top of that list.

Courtney had thought the worst was over after they'd finally reached the reception, but she discovered she was wrong.

She'd forgotten about the first dance.

Not quite knowing what sort of endurance test this was going to be, she braced herself as Gabriel took her hand and led her to the dance floor.

She was pleasantly surprised. His lean, hard body moved as if the music had filled it. Allowing herself to lean into him, Courtney tried to relax. It was a futile effort and that annoyed her. She wasn't accustomed to feeling on edge.

But she was.

"You dance well," she murmured.

And you hold a woman even better. But that part really didn't surprise her. A man who looked like Gabriel had to have had plenty of practice holding a woman. He'd probably been fighting women off for a very long time. She held him accountable for that, too, although she couldn't have easily explained why.

From the look on her face when he had led her to the dance floor, she'd probably expected to have her feet crushed.

John pressed his hand along the small of her back, bringing her closer to him. He could feel his body responding to hers and tried to curb his reaction. But a dead man would have responded to the body that was brushing against his.

"Dancing was invented by the peasant class to entertain themselves. It was one of the few pleasures that the aristocracy couldn't tax out of existence."

Courtney raised her chin defiantly. She wished he wouldn't hold her like that. But there was no way she could pull away from him without causing a scene.

And no way she could block out the feel of his hard body along hers.

"I was giving you a compliment," she retorted between clenched teeth.

He looked down into her face, his expression mildly impassive. "I was giving you history."

She knew exactly what he was up to. He was baiting her, trying to make her angry. And he was succeeding, damn him.

But she couldn't afford that. "There are people present," she admonished in a whisper. "I don't think we should be trying to draw blood so soon after the ceremony."

He curved his hand over hers and rested it against his chest. Maybe he was being a little touchy.

"Sorry." He saw Rick take Mandy's hand and lead her to the floor. At least someone was enjoying himself. "I'm just uncomfortable with this."

That made two of them. "But you did go through with it." Obviously his need for comfort didn't outweigh his desire for money.

There was no reason to tell her that he'd had no choice. That he refused to approach the hospital to consider Katie's surgery as a charity case. He couldn't do that to Katie, not if there was a way out. Instead, he simply nodded. She was vulnerable here, on her home turf, with her lawyer looking on like some medieval gatekeeper. He decided to give her a break.

"Yes, I went through with it and you don't have to worry. I'll live up to my part. And I won't embarrass you."

He was serious, she thought. Maybe he wasn't so bad, after all. "The transfer's been completed," she whispered against his ear.

Her breath warmed him. He had to concentrate to keep his mind on the conversation. "Transfer?"

"The fifty thousand. I had it done just before I left for the church."

He nodded, feeling oddly hollow. But this was why he had gone through with the wedding—the money. No other reasons. "I appreciate that."

"Yes," she murmured. "I know."

He thought she sounded sad, but told himself he was imagining things. She was getting exactly what she wanted: her inheritance with no strings.

He became aware of a clinking sound rising above the soft, bluesy song the orchestra was playing. The din swelled until it all but blotted out the music. He looked over his shoulder at the tables that were scattered around the lush green manicured lawn. Almost all the guests who were seated at them were tapping the backs of their forks against their water glasses.

"Does that mean the same thing in your world that it does in mine?"

He had his answer when she stiffened in his arms.

"Just ignore it."

The noise increased. It was absolutely juvenile, Courtney thought. Whoever came up with the idea of striking water glasses with eating utensils to satisfy some voyeuristic need should have been shot. Well, they could all just go on clinking their glasses until the glasses shattered for all she cared. She wasn't about to perform like some trained monkey in a circus.

If she hadn't actually kissed Gabriel at the altar after the priest had pronounced them husband and wife, she wasn't going to do it now.

John looked down at her face. If he didn't know better, he would have said that Courtney was afraid to kiss him. He found the idea amusing.

"I can ignore it very easily, but I don't think they're going to stop until we give them what they want." He saw Courtney set her mouth stubbornly. John nodded toward the head table. "Don't look now, but I think that your lawyer is getting a tad suspicious about your maidenly reluctance."

Cornered, Courtney blew out breath. There was fire in her eyes when she looked at him. Fire he found even more arousing than the brush of her body along his.

"All right, let's get this over with." Jerking her chin up, Courtney presented her mouth to him. She braced herself for the inevitable.

Or what she thought was the inevitable.

He didn't live up to her expectations.

Or rather, down to them.

Courtney had thought that, in all likelihood, playing the macho man, Gabriel would pull her to him roughly and claim what everyone here thought was his. And in the final analysis, it would just be a matter of skin rubbing along skin, nothing more.

She wasn't prepared for the light touch of his hand as it skimmed along her cheek, wasn't prepared for Gabriel cupping the back of her neck as he tilted her head even more toward him.

And she was nowhere near prepared for the achingly light touch of his lips along hers as they passed first once, then twice, before finally settling and getting down to the business at hand.

Most of all, she wasn't prepared to be swept away and sucked into the heart of a blinding hurricane.

Chapter Six

It began like a ride down a long, slanted chute that was smooth as silk. There were no warning signs posted, no indication of the turbulence—the exhilarating turbulence—that lay just ahead for her.

It caught Courtney completely off guard. Senses lulled, she was taken prisoner in less time than it took to take a breath.

It wasn't a kiss, it was an experience.

Courtney felt almost limp and yet wildly alive as Gabriel's mouth worked over hers, breathing life into her that was unlike anything she'd known. In a matter of seconds, it reduced her from a worldly, sophisticated woman to Alice, propelled into Wonderland and hopelessly lost.

She clutched on to his shoulders for support. Courtney had never felt this disoriented. She wasn't even sure where she was anymore.

Damn, he couldn't do this to her.

He *was* doing this to her.

With almost superhuman effort, she managed to pull herself back up to the surface. Courtney absolutely refused to go down for the third time. Not without taking Gabriel with her.

He felt the explosion the moment it happened. One minute she was pliant, supple in his arms, as weak and as soft as a kitten. The next, it was as if fireworks had suddenly exploded between them. He could feel them.

Fireworks.

A noisy, smoking cherry bomb, all flash and fire. And with the powerful kick of a mule.

John had almost been undone by the sweetness he had tasted when he first pressed his lips to hers. But it was nothing compared to this. This was almost pure rapture. There was passion, anger, raw sensuality.

Everything.

He pressed her body closer to his, completely captivated by the rush that kissing her created.

A deep-rooted sense of reality, of responsibility, fought its way forward. He knew he had to rein himself in before he succumbed and turned this into the three-ring circus he'd abhorred. Before he swept her into his arms, said the hell with the reception and carried Courtney up to her bedroom.

Wherever the hell that was.

Easy? Had he really said that he thought this was going to be easy?

The kiss ended as abruptly as it had flowered, with a mutual pulling back of bodies and lips. Shaken down to their toes, John and Courtney stared at each other in silence. Both had been stunned into speechlessness. Both were worried as hell.

If her heart raced any harder, it was going to leap out of her chest.

"Think that satisfied them?" Was that hoarse voice really coming out of her mouth?

"Ought to." John had to concentrate to push out each word. It wasn't easy. He was too busy concentrating on her. On how her cheeks were suddenly glowing. And how the outline of her mouth was blurred.

If he ran his tongue along his lips, he could still taste her. He stopped suddenly. It wouldn't have been wise to continue.

Though Rick was leading, Mandy managed to maneuver them toward Courtney and John as they danced. Passing them, Mandy inclined her head toward Courtney. "Wow, sure you've got enough fire insurance, Court?" Her eyes glowed with amusement, as well as envy. "For a minute there, I thought we were going to have to turn the hose on you two."

John's eyes shifted toward Rick. Rick was grinning at him, as if he'd just vicariously experienced Courtney's kiss himself.

There was no way to vicariously experience *this,* John thought. The imagination would only pale everything in comparison.

He nodded toward the dance floor. "Keep dancing," John instructed.

"You, too, old friend." Rick looked as if his face was going to split. His glance took them both in before settling on John. "You, too."

As fast as I can, John thought.

"Maybe I'd better see to Katie," he murmured, slipping away from Courtney.

She nodded. Every part of her body had gone numb. Except for her lips. They were throbbing.

"Maybe you'd better," she agreed.

A moment later, their short conversation was a blur. She only vaguely remembered talking to him. She wasn't even sure what she was doing alone on the dance floor.

What the hell had just happened here?

With effort, she collected herself. She had guests to see to. And a wedding reception to host. For now, that was enough to keep her busy.

If she was lucky, her lips would eventually stop throbbing.

"And this," Courtney said, opening the door to the bedroom, "is where you'll sleep."

She paused, watching Katie's face for her reaction. Wanting to make the transition from one home to another as easy as possible for the little girl, Courtney had called in a decorator who specialized in children's rooms. She'd offered the woman triple her fee if she could have the room ready in less than a week. The decorator had finished the job with a day to spare.

Money, Courtney thought, always worked miracles. After all, it had bought her a child as well as a husband. Two for the price of one.

Katie peered into the room, too awestruck to enter. "It's pink," she breathed in wonder.

Very gently, Courtney placed her hand on Katie's back and ushered the little girl into the room. "Yes, I know. Your favorite color."

John was close behind. Too close, in Courtney's estimation, but that was something she was going to have to learn how to deal with. Turning, she saw the surprise on his face.

"You remembered?"

Courtney shrugged, looking away. She didn't quite trust herself to look at him for more than a moment just yet. The reception had been over for less than half an hour, and Gabriel had quickly changed into something far more his speed, jeans and a casual green pullover shirt. He looked more comfortable dressed this way. And far more comfortable than she felt.

She'd changed into shorts and a tank top. There was no honeymoon to rush off to. She didn't think the charade had to be carried that far.

It was bad enough carrying it as far as she was.

"It wasn't that difficult a feat," she finally answered Gabriel. Courtney smiled down at Katie. It was a lot easier talking to her. And a great deal less stressful. "Pink was my favorite color as a kid, too."

"I'm glad," Katie piped up. "That makes us more alike."

Not hardly, John thought. He watched his daughter as Katie walked around the room. It was three times as large as her own bedroom and it certainly looked like a little girl's idea of heaven. There were toys and books everywhere. There was even a television set with its own VCR.

The mark of the affluent, John mused sarcastically.

But what really caught his eyes was the tall Victorian dollhouse standing on the floor beside the window seat. It was the only thing in the room that didn't look as if it had just come straight out of a box. Curious, John crossed to the dollhouse and examined it.

He was right—it wasn't new. Moreover, it appeared to be handmade. Looking at it more closely, he saw rough edges, and there were places where pieces didn't quite fit. The paint was slightly faded and here and there tiny chips were missing. Bare wood peered out from beneath.

It looked completely out of step with the rest of the room and yet, somehow, it was the focal point. The lady was a bit more complex than he'd thought.

John raised a quizzical brow as he glanced in Courtney's direction.

Courtney could feel her hackles rising. He *would* zero in on that.

"It was mine," she explained guardedly. If he said one disparaging word about the dollhouse, she'd make sure he regretted it. "My father gave it to me for my fifth birthday. There were other presents, but this was the one I loved the best." Coming closer, she ran her hand along the gabled roof. "He made it for me. Building things was a hobby of his. Mother said he worked on this for six months."

He wondered if she knew that her eyes softened when she looked at the dollhouse. Probably not.

John nodded, studying the work. "It shows." Touching the door with the tip of his finger, he found that it still worked. He closed the tiny door. "Actually, it shows more than that."

"Oh?" An edge entered her voice. Here it came, the mighty carpenter critiquing the layman's effort. Courtney braced herself, placing a hand on the roof.

His eyes met hers. She seemed ready to go at it at the drop of a hat. "It shows love."

The wind seeped out of her sails. All right, she allowed, so maybe he did have a nice bone or two in his body.

"Yes, it does," Courtney agreed tersely. He clearly knew that she'd been ready to jump down his throat.

Embarrassed, she turned toward Katie. "So, do you like your new room?"

She was prepared to bring in another decorator if Katie found something wanting. That was the way her father had handled all her complaints. With a checkbook and a battery of experts.

And love, Courtney reminded herself. Lots of love. No check could have ever covered that.

Katie turned around, taking one long, panoramic look. "It's wonderful." She turned her face up to Courtney. "Can I sleep here?"

"Of course. And play here," Courtney assured her. She noticed that Gabriel seemed to be hovering over the little girl, as if he was afraid that she was going to do something he didn't want her to. He'd been like that at the reception, as well. What was he worried about? Why didn't he give the child some room to breathe?

Courtney sat down on the canopied bed and patted the space beside her, looking at Katie. Quick to respond, Katie wiggled up on the bed and sat down next to her. Amused by the open, sweet face, Courtney couldn't resist putting her arm around Katie's shoulders. She missed the look that passed over Gabriel's face.

"We can move all your things in here in the morning." Courtney looked at Gabriel. "Yours, too, of course."

"Of course," he echoed her tone and earned a frown for his effort.

Katie looked at her eagerly. "My bed, too?"

She'd been assured that the bed she had purchased for Katie was the very best that money could buy. It was a lot like the one she'd slept in at Katie's age. Courtney glanced up at the canopy.

"Don't you like this bed?"

Like an adult, Katie was quick to soothe any ruffled feathers. "It's a very pretty bed, but my daddy made the one in my room. My old room," she amended.

The child was a born diplomat. Courtney smiled, feathering her hand over the silken head. She knew adults who possessed less finesse and thoughtfulness.

"We'll have your bed in here by tomorrow afternoon. Okay?"

Katie beamed, pleased and relieved. "Okay."

That settled, she scooted off the bed to take one final inventory of the room's treasures.

Katie was examining the contents of the mahogany toy box. That left them alone on the other side of the room. Feeling suddenly awkward, Courtney rose.

"So." She brushed off her hands, though there was nothing there to brush off. Courtney dropped them to her side. "I guess that's it for the tour." She stepped into the hall, expecting Gabriel to follow. Pointing, she indicated the next room down the hall. "That's your room."

The light caught in her hair, flashing a bright red and green. John smiled. When they'd left the church, her friends had thrown confetti instead of rice. Some of it was still in her hair. Without thinking, he reached over and gently extricated it.

He was going to kiss her again. Her breath catching in her throat, Courtney backed away.

She looked like a deer frozen in the headlights of an oncoming car. Why? Was she afraid of him? Or something else?

John opened his hand and showed her the confetti he'd taken from her hair. Embarrassment flashed over her face. The pink hue was oddly arousing. Or maybe it was the vivid memory of the kiss at the reception. No matter what he thought of her, it was going to take him a while to work that through his system.

"And your room?" he asked. "In case someone asks me."

Unable to remain standing so close to him any longer, Courtney began to move down the hall. "No one'll ask. Everyone in the house knows where my room is."

Courtney laced her fingers together, damning herself for feeling so fidgety. There was absolutely no reason to feel like a ball of yarn that had gone tumbling down the hill, unraveling with each revolution.

No reason at all. She could buy and sell him a hundred times over.

Once seemed to be more than enough.

She stopped before her room. "If you must know, this is it. The rooms are adjoining. We share the bathroom and dressing area." She gestured toward the space in between. "I suggest locking the door when you're using either of them."

He didn't care for the habit she had of issuing orders. "Don't worry." She was obviously uncomfortable with the entire arrangement. He would have thought her too sophisticated to be this edgy. "I assume you've seen a naked man before."

He was enjoying this, wasn't he? She wasn't paying him to enjoy himself, just to serve a purpose.

"Only when I've wanted to," she replied crisply. *So don't hold your breath.* Courtney pressed her lips together. There was nothing left to be said. "Well, good night."

"Good night." He inclined his head, taking his leave. And then he added, "One day down, seven hundred and twenty-nine to go."

She stared at him, surprised. She knew why this arrangement felt so intolerable for her, but he should have been reveling in it, in being thrust into the lap of luxury. "You counted?"

"I counted." There was a hint of mocking in his expression. "After all, I wouldn't want to overstay my welcome."

Her eyes narrowed. Her discomfort left, chased away by annoyance. "Don't worry, there's no chance of that. I'll tell you when to go—and where."

He laughed as the fire entered her eyes. This was more like it. "I've no doubts of that. No doubts at all."

Turning abruptly, she slammed her door behind her, then leaned against it, glaring.

Bastard. What right did he have to mock her? He'd never had it so good.

It took more than a moment for Courtney to get a grip on her fury. It was amazing how Gabriel could find exactly the right buttons to push with apparently no effort at all.

She bit her lip. His taste came back to her. Even after all this time and two glasses of champagne, she could still taste him. If she closed her eyes, she could even smell him, that light, spicy scent. Realizing that left her more shaken than angry.

This was never going to work.

Finally, common sense began to seep in, quelling the fire in her breast.

It had to work, she told herself. It was working already. Parsons appeared to be completely taken in at the reception. He even said something about sending them a wedding gift now that he had witnessed the ceremony. Watching her hang on Gabriel's arm, the old curmudgeon obviously thought she had finally gotten serious.

And she was. Serious about keeping what was morally

hers. And it wasn't as if they weren't married. They were. She had the paper—and the thorn in her side, she thought, glancing moodily behind her at the door—to prove it.

Courtney drew in a long breath and then let it out again slowly. They were just going to have to find a way to get along for the next two years.

Or, barring that, interact as little as possible.

Out of sight, out of mind. Courtney laughed softly to herself. That was probably the best way to go. She knew plenty of marriages where the parties involved saw each other only a handful of times a month. It certainly cut down on the arguments.

It didn't do a hell of a lot for their love life, of course; but then, she wasn't in this for a love life.

And neither was Gabriel. All he wanted was the money. The thought left her vaguely angry, though she didn't understand why. There was no reason to be angry. At least they both knew where their priorities were. No lies, no pretenses other than the one they displayed for the world.

Not like with Andrew, she thought ruefully. Andrew Beaudeaux, tall, dark and handsome, blessed with a silver tongue and hypnotic blue eyes. Andrew, who had professed to adore the ground she walked on. She'd been so head over heels in love with him, it had taken her longer than it should have to realize that he only worshipped the ground she walked on only as long as she walked in designer originals across country club terrain.

And after Andrew, there'd been Derrick Evans. Different name, different face, same goals, same motivation. Same small, mercenary souls.

Twice burned, she'd put away the matches and decided to live for the moment. To enjoy herself without any thought to having a future with her companion of choice. Her companion of the moment. They rarely lasted longer than a few weeks. No men were worth heartache. And they certainly weren't worth feeling inadequate about herself.

There was a great deal more to her than just a bankbook or an estate, she thought fiercely. But she no longer cared about trying to get that point across. And certainly not to the likes of John Gabriel.

Courtney ran her hand along the back of her neck, wishing herself two years into the future and out of this situation her father had placed her in.

A fragment of a memory floated through her mind, whispering seductively. Her fingertips feathered along the back of her neck, just as Gabriel's had this afternoon at the reception.

Just before he had kissed her.

They'd kissed each other, she thought stubbornly, forcing the air back into her lungs. And she had given as good as she'd got—after Gabriel had gotten off the first salvo.

Funny how she thought of the kiss in terms of a declaration of war, or an act of aggression. It hadn't felt like that actually. Not if she really thought about it.

It had felt...

Courtney could feel her blood heating as it flowed through her veins.

No, she wasn't going to do that to herself. It would be playing right into his hands. He could act highhanded about the situation and mock her, but she knew better. She saw through him just as she had eventually seen through the others. There was just one main difference. She wasn't in love with Gabriel, the way she had been with Andrew and then Derrick. With the exception of her mother and father, she didn't believe in love anymore.

Annoyed with herself, with her father and, most of all, with Gabriel, Courtney walked out of her room again. She needed some air.

The door to Katie's room was still standing wide open, its light mingling with the light in the hall. She could hear Gabriel's voice. He was talking to his daughter.

No, she thought, listening. He was reading to her. Gabriel must have picked up one of the storybooks from the bookshelf.

Courtney turned to go to the other stairway, then stopped. The deep, rhythmic cadence of Gabriel's voice as he read to his child drew her in as surely as if she were a fish being reeled in by a first-class fisherman.

Courtney approached the room quietly, not wanting to intrude or make her presence known. She stopped just shy of the door and listened.

Recognition was instantaneous. *The Cat in the Hat.*

A soft, fond smile spread on her lips. Her father had read the same story to her.

Without realizing it, Courtney leaned against the wall and wrapped her arms around herself. A sense of incredible peace descended over her. She could remember lying in her bed with her father sitting on the chair beside her. He read to her every night. His deep, rumbly voice made the words sound as if they were engraved in time-worn stone.

Memories drifted back. Warm, treasured memories.

She'd been much happier then, she realized with a pang. Genuinely happy instead of this phony jet-setting happiness she'd talked herself into.

Back then she had known who loved her, who mattered. Honesty wasn't something she had to go looking for. It had been a part of her life every day. Just as her father had been.

She realized that she hadn't really felt safe and warm since her father had died.

Courtney smiled ruefully to herself. She would have cut out anyone's tongue for saying the same to her, but in the recesses of her mind, she could admit it. Sometimes, just sometimes, she needed someone to hold her and tell her everything was all right.

Just as Gabriel was doing with Katie.

She sighed to herself. Maybe he wasn't so bad, after all. Maybe...

Startled, Courtney straightened as Gabriel came out of the bedroom. He looked as surprised to see her as she was to be seen.

"Um, I came to see if there was anything else she needed." Courtney struggled to sound nonchalant. She hated being caught off guard like this. "I know how disorienting all this must be to her."

John eased the door shut behind him. He'd worried about Katie a lot today. All this had to be particularly taxing for her. But Katie had surprised him by bearing up well. Maybe the doctor was being unduly pessimistic about her condition. Maybe they could hold off a little longer until she was older, stronger.

In the meantime, he'd bank the money this stint in hell was earning him.

Maybe that was a little harsh. Courtney's thoughtfulness toward his daughter made him reassess his opinion of her. Maybe she wasn't quite the spoiled brat he thought her to be.

"Actually, I think she's adjusting to this better than we are. She's very adaptable."

Courtney just wanted to get back to her own room. "Good, it's a quality she's going to need in life."

John frowned. She didn't have a clue as to what Katie did or didn't need. "Katie has everything she needs."

There was that protectiveness again, Courtney thought. Katie was a child, not a possession. She shrugged. It wasn't any business of hers.

John closed his hand around the doorknob. "Well, good night again."

"Good night." Courtney backed away. Breeding prompted her to ask, "You don't need anything, do you?"

Like what? What was she magnanimously going to offer him now? "What more could I want than this?" John gestured about the house.

No, she'd been right to begin with. Gabriel was insufferable. Just because he read bedtime stories to his daughter, that didn't make him a prince. That barely made him likable.

"Nothing," she retorted.

Courtney spun around on her heel. The click of her door was followed by the sound of his being shut.

She blinked her eyes furiously. Hell of a way to spend a wedding night, she thought. The moisture on her lashes dripped down her cheeks.

Chapter Seven

The noise woke her, penetrating her consciousness like a pneumatic drill.

Courtney firmly believed that mornings were God's way of exacting punishment for mankind's transgressions. As far as she was concerned, days should start at a decent hour. Like ten or eleven. Or, if absolutely necessary, nine.

With effort, she pried open her eyes. Daylight assaulted her, bathing her room with bold strokes of amber and gold.

Instincts of self-preservation had Courtney pulling the pillow over her head. The alarm clock continued its shrill ringing. With a groan, she tossed the pillow aside and glared at the clock.

Seven o'clock. Exactly what she had set it for. She must have been out of her mind.

Edwin Parsons had told her that unless she wanted to

wait three weeks, the only possible time he could bring her the papers she needed to sign was before he went to his office. For the past thirty years, Parsons had always been at his desk by eight.

Why not? He had no life, she thought miserably. The man was married to his career. All he cared about was work. She, on the other hand, cared about a great many things, none of which involved getting up at an ungodly hour. But, not wanting to wait any longer than necessary, Courtney had agreed to the time.

Now she sorely regretted it. She needed to be reasonably alert when Parsons arrived, as well as showered and dressed.

That meant getting out of bed.

She wondered if it was too late to call Parsons and tell him to stop by some night this week after work, no matter how late.

Probably. Resigned, Courtney dragged herself up into a sitting position. She felt exhausted. More so than she'd been in a long time. Getting less than four hours' sleep would do that to a person.

Insomnia wasn't usually her bedmate, but it had been last night. The hours had stretched themselves before her, moving minute by slow, torturously long minute, until they had knitted themselves into an inky black cloak that threatened to strangle her.

It was no mystery what had sent her on the journey into the depths of sleeplessness. The same thing that was bothering her now. She was married. Married to someone she didn't know, didn't even like. Someone who, because of nature's perverse sense of humor, she was physically attracted to to such a degree that it nearly robbed her of her senses.

If that wasn't cause for insomnia, she didn't know

what was. Just thinking of being tied to that smug, muscle-bound—

No, she wasn't going to think about it, or him. She was just going to do what she had to in order to get through this charade. She'd endured worse. She'd endured finding out that as far as the men she loved were concerned, her main asset—maybe her only one—was her money. Compared to that, this was a cakewalk.

Well, maybe not a cakewalk, but easier.

And two years would be gone soon enough, as would he. Look at how quickly her life had flown by so far, she thought ruefully. There was a time when thirty seemed like eternity away. Now it was a matter of a little more than two weeks.

She'd make it, Courtney promised herself. Besides, it wasn't two years anymore. It was two years minus one day.

Courtney stopped as she remembered. That was exactly the way Gabriel had described the remaining time last night.

Their wedding night.

The alarm clock began ringing again. It was set to go off at three-minute intervals until she shut it off. Doubling her hand into a fist, she brought it down on the buzzer. It fell into silence. It also fell off the nightstand. Satisfaction brought a small smile to her lips. Courtney left the clock on the floor.

Satisfaction was short-lived, disappearing before her feet touched the floor. Maybe a shower would help. A nice, cold shower to coax her back among the living. She couldn't face Parsons like this. One look at her bleary-eyed face and he'd know she wasn't the blissful bride.

She didn't have to be blissful, Courtney reminded herself. She just had to be a bride.

Of a Neanderthal.

Still more than half-asleep, Courtney stumbled through her bedroom toward the dressing room and the bathroom that lay just beyond it. The crumpled white heap in the corner assumed the shape of her discarded wedding gown as she approached it.

The sight of the gown caused her throat to tighten. Almost everyone at the reception had told her what a beautiful bride she made. Too bad she hadn't felt beautiful. Or happy.

Courtney picked up the gown and laid it carefully on the unmade bed. Maybe next time, she thought. Maybe next time it would be for real.

With the heel of her hand, she wiped away a tear and called herself a fool.

Preoccupied, Courtney didn't see him until she had closed the door behind her and turned around. Looking back on it later, it seemed incredible that she hadn't seen Gabriel when she'd first walked in.

Once she was aware of him, Courtney couldn't see anything else *but* Gabriel. And she became conscious of a wild, rushing sound in her ears. It matched the pace created by her heart.

Any second now, she was sure that God's voice would break in, announcing: "This is a test, this is merely a test." Because Gabriel was standing in front of her almost naked.

Stray beads of water from the shower he'd just taken were still clinging to his shoulders and his torso. That was practically all that was clinging to him, beyond her gaze. He had very little else on, save for a towel that in her estimation was only a little larger than a standard washcloth.

You could wash laundry on his stomach, she thought, a strange sensation registering in her knees. The same sensation that she'd felt last night when he kissed her.

Courtney's startled gasp made him jump. John swung away from the mirror, the toothbrush slipping from his fingers. Picking it up, he looked at Courtney. His body temperature went up ten degrees.

Since when had they started making nightgowns out of spider webs? The one Courtney had on was hardly thicker than cellophane, at least in this light. Unable to help himself, John allowed his eyes to drift appreciatively over her. He might not be crazy about the lady's high-handed manner and her less than winning personality, but he certainly had no complaints when it came to the way she looked. The lady was very easy on the eyes. And hard on a man who wanted no entanglements.

The light coming from the dressing room behind her moved along her body like a lover's hand, bringing attention to the supple curves just in case he had missed them.

He hadn't.

Knowing he had to speak before he completely swallowed his tongue, John tried to downplay his reaction. He turned his back on Courtney. The mist on the mirror obscured her just enough for him to function.

He poured water into his cup. "You're staring. What's wrong? This isn't your toothbrush, in case you're wondering."

The hem of her nightgown brushed along her thigh, reminding Courtney just how short it was. She wished she'd thought to put on a robe. But then, Gabriel wasn't supposed to have been in here. He was supposed to have obeyed the rules.

Just what she needed, a rebel.

Like her.

Courtney crossed her arms before her. Pride prevented her from making a grab for the towel on the rack to cover up. She'd just have to brazen this out.

Her eyes narrowed accusingly. "You're supposed to lock the door when you're in here."

Her critical tone brought back memories. None of them pleasant. "It's early." He rinsed, then spat. Setting the cup down, his eyes met hers in the mirror. "I didn't think your kind got up before noon."

"My kind?" she echoed. Her eyebrows rose so high, they nearly touched her hairline. Anger filled her like a rough, physical entity. Who the hell did he think he was, lumping her with others as if she were a playing card to be shuffled into a deck?

Furious, she raised her chin. "What would you know about 'my kind'?"

It was a poor choice of words, but he was too annoyed at her tone to apologize. Her chin made a nice target. He ignored it and congratulated himself on his restraint. When he trusted his voice to answer her, it was low, and dangerous.

"I was married to one of 'your kind.'"

The admission stopped her cold. She hadn't known that. It suddenly occurred to Courtney that there was a great deal she didn't know about this man who was standing almost naked in her bathroom. About the only thing she *did* know was that any woman under the age of ninety would have gladly paid to be in her place.

His words hung between them like a damp shower curtain, heavy and murky. She thought of the bright-eyed child who'd asked her to be her mommy. It was her that Courtney's heart went out to.

"Katie's mother?"

He didn't like talking about Diane, especially not with a stranger, but Courtney managed to get him so angry so fast—

With effort, he banked down his emotions. "Katie's mother," he acknowledged.

"And she was…" Her voice trailed off as she looked for the right words. "Well off?"

Maybe he did this sort of a thing for a living, she thought suddenly. A good-looking carpenter offering a broad shoulder to cry on to emotionally vulnerable women. It wasn't an implausible scenario.

No, that wasn't fair. She'd been the one to approach him, not the other way around. But maybe that was part of his technique, too. He hadn't exactly waited all that long before accepting her offer, had he?

"Filthy rich." He said the words as if they left a bad taste in his mouth. As if having money tainted someone. He didn't expect her to buy that, did he? After all, that was why he'd entered into this arrangement of theirs. For money. "And now she's dead. End of subject."

She hadn't known that, either. Courtney blew out a breath. Did it upset him to talk about his late wife? Though his tone was curt, she didn't think so. He didn't look as if he'd lost the love of his life. Taking another glance at Gabriel's face, she knew condolences would have been out of order.

But something *had* hurt him, she would have bet anything on it. She'd seen that look before, in her own eyes when she'd glimpsed in the mirror. Feeling awkward, Courtney shrugged. "Sorry."

He didn't want her pity. Just enough of her money to

cover Katie's medical expenses. "Don't be," he said brusquely.

The big jerk, couldn't he accept anything graciously? "I mean I was sorry I brought it up."

She was tired of talking to the back of his head. Hand on his shoulder, Courtney roughly turned him around to face her.

"Look, do you think you could force yourself to speak in complete sentences? Parsons is coming over this morning to see me. Us. Specifically, probably to look you over at close range. He's not expecting much, but I don't want him thinking I married Rambo or Clint Eastwood."

With an economy of movement, he removed her hand from his shoulder, then replaced the toothpaste on the medicine cabinet shelf. "You're mixing your images."

He'd lost her. "What?"

John spared her a glance over his shoulder. God, but he was glad their marriage had a termination clause in it. "It's either Rambo and Dirty Harry, or Sylvester Stallone and Clint Eastwood." Shutting the medicine cabinet, he turned to face her again. "One set is fiction, the other's real."

Now he was critiquing the way she spoke? "You can be very annoying, you know that?"

Without blinking an eye, he leaned over her and answered, "So can you."

He was in her space, crowding her. Affecting her. Courtney was far more aware of him than she was happy about, but she'd be damned if she'd allow him to see it. "Well, we have that in common, don't we?"

She was glaring at him. Her expression in no way undermined the total effect she was having on him. And there was no way John could divorce himself from the fact that the woman's body could have been classified as a lethal weapon.

Knowing it infuriated her, he let his eyes travel up to her face. The journey began at her feet. "Think you could see your way into putting something on?"

Insolent jerk. Courtney couldn't remember when she'd ever felt as physically vulnerable as she did now. Feeling cornered, she lashed out. "Don't you dictate to me."

Dictate? Did she think this was some sort of a power struggle?

"I'm telling you for your own good."

Just because she'd said a few words before an altar and signed a piece of paper—a piece of paper that would be null and void soon enough—didn't give him the right to order her around. She could damn well walk around stark naked if she wanted to. This was her house, not his.

The fact that she knew she was being completely irrational didn't stop her. Gabriel really did bring out the worst in her, she thought.

"Oh, really? For my own good?" Her chin rose pugnaciously. "And why would that be?" Sarcasm filled her voice even as she struggled not to let him get the better of her. "What's going to happen to me if I don't run off like a good little girl and put something on?"

She smelled of sleep, he thought, and something else. Something seductively tempting. As tempting as those breasts she was inadvertently thrusting at him as she issued her challenge.

John clenched his hands at his sides, struggling to hold himself in check. "You might get more than you bargained for."

"From you?" Her eyes narrowed. When threatened,

or afraid, it was best to go on the offensive, and right now, she was a little of both. "I don't think so. I've got your number, Gabriel, and I know exactly what you're capable of."

If it was the last thing he did, he was going to wipe that smug look off her face. "Think again."

It probably *was* going to be the last thing he did, heaven help him. Before she could move out of his way, John caught her by the shoulders and brought her to him, behaving exactly the way he'd always abhorred.

Courtney opened her mouth to upbraid him. To call him every name she could think of. The sound died in her throat, transforming into something that was half curse, half whimper.

This time, there was no prelude, no gentleness to lull her into a false sense of security. No tender touch along her cheek to drug her.

This time, the explosion came immediately, setting her on fire as neatly, as effectively, as if he'd physically struck a match to her.

Suddenly Courtney found her hands winding into his damp hair instead of pushing him away the way she'd intended.

His body was hard, demanding, as it pressed against hers. Her response to that was immediate, too, as if it had been programmed into her. Or, at the very least, preordained. She could feel her body quivering as he molded her to him.

Or was she molding herself to him? The lines blurred. There was only his mouth, his hands, reducing her to a state of almost mindless passion. Her breath evaporated in her lungs, leaving her gasping as she struggled to grab a little more of this ecstasy she'd been tendered.

Greedy for his taste, her mouth worked over his, snuffing out her anger and substituting need in its place.

She hated him for making her want him like this. And she did. She wanted him in the worst way. But the very worst thing she could do was let him suspect how she felt.

How could he not know?

She blocked the thought from her mind, blocked out everything but the sensations that were spiraling through her body as every fiber of her being was drawn into this raw kiss.

He could have devoured her. Damn it, he wanted to hate her, to despise everything she stood for. But he couldn't hate and want at the same time. And his body was in a state of rebellion, turning his mind, his common sense, against him.

Needs were terrible things. They took no prisoners, showed no mercy. He'd wanted to frighten her, to teach her a lesson that he wasn't just some lackey she could bully.

But the only lesson being taught was that he was far more vulnerable in this little setup than she was. For all he knew, this might be business as usual for her.

It damn well wasn't for him.

"Daddy?" The small voice wedged itself between them like a physical entity. "Daddy," Katie called out. "Are you in there?"

They jumped apart as if they'd been seared by a hot branding iron.

Courtney was surprised and relieved to discover that she could actually stand on her own. The last couple of moments in his arms had left her in doubt. The man could kiss like nobody's business.

She dragged air back into her lungs as she looked

toward the door. His daughter couldn't find them here like this.

Glancing one last time at him before she left, Courtney advised, "Your towel's drooping."

The slightest hint of a smile curved his mouth as he tucked the ends more tightly together against his flat stomach. The towel might be drooping, but she'd certainly had a different effect on other parts of him.

"Thanks."

She was backing away, trying not to seem as if she were actually fleeing. But she was. She desperately needed to regroup.

"I'm in here, honey," Gabriel called out.

Turning, Courtney pressed her hand against her stomach. It was fluttering so badly, she fully expected to feel it quaking beneath her palm. The man hadn't even had the decency to have morning breath, she'd thought grudgingly. He'd tasted sweet. Intoxicatingly sweet. And more addictive than the chocolates that heretofore were her main weakness.

"Good morning, Daddy." She heard Katie greet her father just as she slipped out. "Good morning, Mommy." The girl's voice floated behind her.

Courtney stopped dead. The greeting caused something to ache within her. Probably just the oysters from yesterday. There was no reason to make something out of this.

But instead of leaving, Courtney turned around. Katie, already dressed, hurried to her side. Her small face was pinched as worry suddenly creased it.

"Is it okay?" she asked hopefully. "Can I call you Mommy now?"

Oh, God. At a complete loss, Courtney glanced toward Gabriel. "I—"

Katie gave her no opportunity to turn the honor down. "—'cause you married my daddy, so that makes you my new mommy. Jenny calls the lady who married her daddy Claire, but I don't want to call you Court—" She stopped, trying to remember the rest of the long, unfamiliar name. "Court—"

"Courtney," John supplied when Courtney only stared dumbly at his daughter.

He'd set her up for this, he thought, disgusted with himself. It was his fault that Katie was baring her heart to this woman, pouring out all the love she had. Damn it, anyway. He should have tried harder to find the money somewhere else.

John placed a hand on her shoulder, anchoring her to him. Drawing her away from Courtney. "Maybe we're being a little hasty here, honey. I really don't think—"

Courtney ran her tongue along her lips, hesitating. The taste of him only confused the issue further for her. But there was something distant and warm moving within her, filling her heart.

Mommy.

Someone wanted to call her Mommy.

She could remember the ache she'd felt when there'd been no one for her to call Mommy. She'd been older than Katie when her mother had died, but the pain, she knew, was the same no matter what the age.

Courtney placed her hand on Katie's other shoulder. Her eyes met Gabriel's. She had the impression that they were momentarily waging a tug of war. Gabriel raised his hand, stepping back.

She looked down at Katie. "It's all right, Katie. You can call me Mommy if you really want to."

Katie nodded so hard, her hair bobbed up and down. "I *really* want to."

The smile on Katie's face erased any doubts Courtney had. At least for the moment.

When she raised her eyes from the child's beaming face, John was looking at her. There was a strange look in his eyes. For the life of her, Courtney couldn't fathom what he was thinking.

He was probably annoyed with her because he thought she was moving in where she had no business being.

Well, so was he, she thought in frustrated annoyance. Oh, she had asked him to move into her house. But something within her was afraid that Gabriel was moving in somewhere else. A place where *he* had absolutely no business being.

She began to move away again. "Let me know when you're finished in here." Courtney turned to leave.

She heard him turn the water on, then off again. "I'm finished."

And so would she be if she wasn't careful. Courtney pressed her lips together. She had to get hold of herself, she thought. She was beginning to act like a sentimental idiot. The child was just four years old—she would have called any woman Mommy if allowed. It didn't mean anything.

Squaring her shoulders, she looked at him. Had the towel gotten smaller? "You'll put something appropriate on, I hope."

He had to hand it to her, she certainly knew how to ruin a moment. "What's appropriate these days for an interrogation?"

She doubted it would come to that. Parsons had seemed quite taken with Gabriel, the little he had seen of him at the reception.

"Sackcloth and ashes." Her flippant tone matched

his. "But we're fresh out. In lieu of that, try the charcoal gray pin-striped suit."

"I don't own a charcoal gray pin-striped suit."

It was unsettling, standing here and looking at him dressed only in a towel. Moreover, she was sure he knew it. Courtney purposely turned toward Katie. The little girl seemed content just listening to them. She couldn't help wondering just how much Katie was absorbing.

"Yes, you do," she informed him. She led the way back into the dressing room to show him. "It's next to the beige Armani."

He'd just assumed that the clothes in the closet belonged to a former lover who had left too quickly to pack. Probably running for his life. He looked around. There were more suits here than in a department store— and enough ties to outfit a battalion of kites, which was all he thought ties were good for. Just looking at them made his throat close up.

"You've been busy."

"The buyer was." She'd issued a list of instructions, along with sizes she had obtained from Gabriel under duress. The men's shop on Rodeo Drive that her father had favored had done the rest.

Courtney pulled out the suit in question and held it up against him. She had to admit that part of her preferred him in the towel. "Can't have my husband looking like he just stepped out of a thrift shop, now, can I?"

Katie tugged on the hem of her nightgown. "Want me to go change, too?"

Gabriel could stand to take lessons in cooperation from his daughter. "You," Courtney said, sliding a fingertip down the pert nose, "are perfect just the way you are."

With that, she turned and walked out, knowing that Gabriel was watching her. Though she knew it was a cheap trick, Courtney swayed her hips just a little.

Chapter Eight

"Courtney? What are you doing calling me? I didn't expect to hear from you so soon."

It had been almost two weeks since the wedding. Whenever they were both in town, she and Mandy usually got together about once a week. Courtney couldn't see why her friend seemed so surprised that she was calling.

"What do you mean, 'so soon'? I haven't talked to you in over a week and a half."

Mandy's laugh was deep and sultry as she let her imagination wander. "And what a week and a half it's probably been. Don't think I haven't envied you. I just didn't think you'd come up for air for a while, that's all."

Mandy was carrying her joke too far. And it was no longer funny. "I got married, Mandy. I didn't become a deep-sea diver."

Mandy began to laugh again, but then stopped abruptly. "Court, you're not trying to tell me that you and he haven't—"

How had she gotten sidetracked like this? She'd called Mandy to invite her to a party this Saturday night. A party that might help take her mind off the tension that had become her constant companion. Tension that was generated precisely by the lack of what Mandy was alluding to.

"No, we haven't," she retorted more sharply than she'd intended.

The silence on the other end of the line stretched out until Courtney thought they'd been disconnected. When Mandy finally spoke, her voice was almost solemn. "Courtney, I've never known you to be stupid before."

Courtney sat down on the edge of the desk, cradling the telephone in her lap. From her vantage point, she could see the guest house. He was out there again, working. Just as he had been every day since the wedding.

At least he had a way to release his frustration, she thought grudgingly. She wondered if he'd let her hammer something.

Mandy's comment did nothing to improve her mood. "It's a business arrangement, nothing more. Remember?" Mandy knew why she'd married Gabriel. She'd been the one to suggest it in the first place. Why did she suddenly sound as if it was a love match? If anything, it was a grudge match. On both their parts.

Courtney sighed. What she really needed was to get away. But how would it look to go somewhere so soon without her husband? And taking him along negated the reason for going in the first place. Besides, the foundation's annual fund-raiser was coming up soon. She was the hostess and she couldn't just abandon that because she was uncomfortable about her living conditions. There were too many children who depended on that foundation. Children, she mused watching Gabriel's little girl, who deserved a chance to be as well as Katie was.

"Business, huh?" How could Courtney be letting such a great opportunity slip through her fingers? "Ever hear of mixing business with pleasure? If it were me in your place, that man would have been reduced to a liquid state by now, pouring himself out of my bed every morning."

Courtney sincerely doubted that. If anything, Gabriel was the reducer, not the reducee. But that was something Mandy didn't need to know.

She leaned forward on the desk to get a better look. Didn't the man ever work in a shirt? Frustrated by the effect the sight of his sweaty chest had on her, she turned away.

Within a couple of seconds, she found herself turning back again. "There is no pleasure with living with an overbearing, monosyllabic man, Mandy." The tight, wet knot in her stomach bore her out.

Mandy's laugh told her she knew better. "Oh, I don't know. I could find pleasure."

Mandy could find pleasure dating an eight-by-ten glossy. But Courtney needed more than that. She needed substance. A man who treated her tenderly. And who didn't give a damn if her bank account was in the single digits or more than seven.

Courtney disregarded the deep sigh she heard in the receiver. "If it wasn't for the way he treats his daughter, I wouldn't think he was human at all."

"He looks plenty human to me—and there are ways to test that theory." Courtney could almost see Mandy's eyes gleaming. "Want me to go over them with you? Better yet, want me to demonstrate?"

She didn't have time to listen to this. If this party was to come off on such short notice, she had lists to make and people to contact.

"No, I just want you to come to my party. I'm inviting all my friends to officially introduce my husband. Sort of a coming-out party." It was also her birthday, but turning thirty wasn't something she wanted to celebrate. Not when she had an albatross around her neck.

"Ah, a cozy evening at home with only the immediate world in attendance." There was nothing Mandy loved more than a party, except for Courtney. "Really, Court, do you think that's wise? Showing him off? Some of the women we know will jump at the chance to try to lure him away—and not just because he's yours, this time. The man is drop-to-your-knees-and-thank-your-lucky-stars gorgeous. It's like smearing your hand with goose pâté and sticking it into a tank full of piranhas."

"They can lure him away all they want after the paperwork for the trust fund is signed and the money is transferred into my account."

It was on the tip of Mandy's tongue to quote Shakespeare's line about the lady protesting too much, but she let it go. She knew just how far Courtney's patience stretched.

"Uh-huh. Remember who your best friend is when you're having your garage sale."

Mandy was hopeless, she thought. Normally, Courtney found her humor infectious. Right now, it was only irritating.

Everything was irritating lately. Even getting her own way. She was beginning to feel like a disgruntled shrew. That was Gabriel's fault, too.

"When this is over, I won't sell him to you, I'll make you a present of him." *I'll even throw in a spare shirt,* she thought, watching the way the perspiration made his body glow in the afternoon heat.

Didn't he have enough sense to come in out of the sun?

She was letting her mind wander again. Courtney forced herself to concentrate on what Mandy was saying.

"—not that I wouldn't sell my soul for the man, but I don't think he'll come all that willingly."

A lot Mandy knew. "Yes, he will. He's already chomping at the bit."

"Yeah, but which way is that bit pointing?" Silence on the other end told Mandy that Courtney didn't understand. "Hey, I saw the way he looked at you when you were dancing at the reception. And that kiss—"

Courtney didn't want to hear about it. "Done for effect, Mandy. Nothing more."

Even special effects had their limits, Mandy thought, and what she'd witnessed had seemed genuine enough from where she had stood. Why was Courtney being so stubborn? She would have killed to have a man like that within her reach. "Well, it sure affected me. I lived off the fumes for a week."

Enough was enough. "Party. Saturday. Eight. Formal. Be there."

"With bells on," she promised, then added wistfully, "Maybe if I'm lucky, he'll ring one or two."

She hoped Mandy would stop beating this dead horse by the time she came to the party. "Goodbye, Mandy."

Courtney hung up and sighed. Her gaze drifted toward the guest house. Gabriel was doing something to a door he had brought out and leaned against a sawhorse. Even at this distance, she was aware of the way the muscles on his back rippled as he worked.

She blinked, suddenly realizing that she was staring. It wasn't as if she'd never seen a man without his shirt on before. It was just that, she had to admit, she had never seen anyone quite so perfect-looking before.

Courtney didn't relish telling him that his services were required. She didn't relish having to tell him anything at all. The more distance between them, the better chance this charade of theirs had of working.

Although, she had to admit that the dinners they'd shared so far were not as bad as she'd anticipated. They ate as a family strictly for Katie's sake and any conversations they had were centered around the child. There had been a few eye-opening moments that gave her a glimpse of what their life together was like. Gabriel wasn't quite the self-serving clod she'd envisioned him to be.

That still didn't make this easy.

Courtney sighed again as she got off the desk. She hoped he'd be more cooperative this time. When he'd come down to greet Parsons that first morning, he'd put on his usual jeans and shirt instead of the suit she'd asked him to wear. He'd been deliberately defiant. The smile she'd seen in his eyes told her that he enjoyed pressing her buttons.

He'd pressed more by acting the part of the enamored husband, touching her hair, slipping his arm around her shoulder. He'd done it so well, even she might have been taken in—if she hadn't known better.

The meeting had gone off far better than she'd hoped. Parsons had left, promising to begin transferring the initial sum into her account by noon.

"There'll be an equal transfer in a year," he'd told

her as he reached the front door. "The balance, of course, will remain in abeyance until the end of the second year."

"Of course," she'd echoed. She knew better now than to secretly hope the old man might be persuaded to revert the entire trust to her account in one transaction.

She remembered Parsons looking past her, at Gabriel, who had remained in the living room with Katie. One of the few smiles she'd ever seen gracing his lined face made an appearance.

"I guess your father really did know best in this matter. He seems to be a fine young man."

"All this from a few words?" She could keep the sarcasm from her tongue, but not the words themselves.

The small eyes had looked at her knowingly. "The investigator's report was more than a few words, Mrs. Gabriel."

She'd stared at him, dumbfounded, forgetting to remind Parsons that she was keeping her maiden name. "Report?"

His manner, though not condescending, had been patronizing. "Yes. You don't think your father would have wanted you marrying a serial killer just to satisfy a clause in his will, do you? His instructions to me were to have the prospective groom thoroughly investigated before the wedding." The thin shoulders moved beneath the jacket that seemed to have grown too large for him with time. "Granted, it was a rush job. Your invitation didn't leave the investigator much time to do his work, but it was more than adequate." He summed it up tersely. "I feel that I know all I need to know."

But she didn't. There were gaping holes in Gabriel's background, so much she didn't know. "About the report. Could I see it?"

The small eyes had all but penetrated her. For a moment, it almost seemed as if he could read her thoughts. Did he suspect that the marriage was a sham?

"Why would you have to? You can ask Mr. Gabriel anything you want to know. He is, after all, an honest man."

She'd nodded, retreating. Gabriel volunteered nothing and she refused to ask him anything outright. To do so would have only made her seem unduly curious.

But she *was* curious, Courtney thought now as she stared out the French doors. Curious why a man who professed to have graduated with a degree in engineering from UCLA had been earning a living renovating a guest house.

Curious why a man who claimed to have married into a family of social prominence had all but sold himself into what amounted to servitude for two years for a sum that would have been thought of as petty cash by many people.

Why had he turned himself into an indentured servant when he supposedly had other resources?

He certainly didn't look like an indentured servant from here. She watched him set the door aside, and then bring out another one. His biceps bulged.

Mandy would have left drool marks from here to the pool if she could have seen him. As for that first morning's encounter in the bathroom, she doubted Mandy's heart could have withstood it.

Courtney could feel her own skin warming just thinking about it.

Just as it did when she lay in her bed at night, wondering what it would be like to have her new husband make love with her.

She shook her head. Nothing that looked that good could possibly live up to its packaging.

But that didn't stop her from wondering what it would be like. Or why he hadn't made another move toward her since that first morning.

Didn't he find her attractive? Wasn't she even worth an effort?

At this rate, she wasn't going to survive two years. She was going to make herself crazy inside of a month and then it wouldn't matter who got the inheritance.

Squaring her shoulders, Courtney threw open the French doors and walked out. The sound of Katie's laughter floated lightly through the air on the summer breeze. Courtney couldn't help smiling. The sound never failed to create a feeling of well-being within her. Katie was the perfect antidote to her father.

As she approached, Courtney saw that Katie was playing on the lawn with the puppy she'd impulsively bought for her last week. It was a consolation gift because Katie had missed Mandy's poodle after Cuddles had gone home.

Katie was lying on the grass, having her face washed by a fast-moving pink tongue. The dog, Squiggles, a black toy poodle, was doing a thorough job.

His back to the main house, Gabriel tensed. She was coming. He couldn't hear Courtney's approach over the noise Katie and the puppy were making, but the breeze had just shifted and he could detect the lightest bit of her perfume.

It was enough to alert him. And arouse him.

The drill bit suddenly punctured the wood, going farther than he'd planned. He stifled a curse. With a little wood putty strategically applied, it could be fixed. But it shouldn't have had to be fixed. You would have thought, he mused in disgust, that a man his age wouldn't have to go through this kind of garbage.

Maybe it was just the stress of worrying about Katie getting to him.

He knew better than to lie to himself. He'd gone down that road once, lied to himself to ignore the obvious. And all that had accomplished was to postpone the inevitable. The truth always had a way of coming out and bringing consequences along with it.

Courtney watched his back as Gabriel worked. Even his body language shut her out. It looked like a solid, flesh wall. She'd done some shutting out of her own. Since the morning after the wedding, she had gone out of her way to avoid Gabriel as much as possible, except for dinner. She might have succeeded, too, if not for Katie. Katie seemed determined to wiggle her way into her life.

She already had.

Scrambling up into a sitting position, Katie sent the dog tumbling over on its side, a mass of paws and ears.

"Mommy, you're up." She looked overjoyed to see her. At least someone was, Courtney thought, glancing at Gabriel again. "Daddy said not to bother you, so I didn't."

Courtney sat down beside Katie on the lawn. The puppy began sniffing at her sandals. "Thank you. I like to sleep in."

Squiggles started nipping at her toes. Courtney yelped and Katie tugged the dog over toward her. The animal moved in a boneless heap, reminding Courtney of a cat she'd once had.

"Why don't you sleep with Daddy?"

Courtney's head snapped up. Katie's innocent question brought an abrupt end to her nostalgic journey.

"Jenny's new mommy sleeps with her daddy," Katie persisted.

Wasn't four too young to ask questions like this? At a loss, Courtney looked toward Gabriel for help.

John was accustomed to Katie's inquisitive mind, though it had never taken such a personal direction before. "Your new mommy kicks when she's asleep." He could see that Courtney didn't care for his explanation, but it was the best he could come up with on short notice. He grinned at his daughter. "And I don't like getting bruised."

"And your daddy snores," she countered, "so I can't sleep. Having two separate bedrooms is more restful for everybody." Courtney looked at him pointedly.

"Oh." Katie accepted the explanation without question. A moment later she was immersed in a tug-of-war with Squiggles over her sneaker. Giggling, she jumped up and began to chase after the dog.

John dropped his hammer into the opened toolbox. "Katie," he called her name sternly. "You know what I said about running around."

With a sigh, Katie stopped instantly. Turning, she walked slowly back to him.

Courtney glared at Gabriel. Just what was his problem? Didn't he want to see anyone have fun? Annoyed, she got up and chased after the puppy.

Katie's gleeful shouts of encouragement rang in her ears as she managed to corner Squiggles between the guest house wall and one leg of the sawhorse.

"Gotcha!" Holding the squirming bundle of fluff against her, Courtney brought the puppy and Katie's sneaker back to the little girl. "There you go, pumpkin."

Taking him, Katie stumbled beneath the burden before righting herself. Courtney saw Gabriel reach for his daughter, then stop when she didn't fall. He looked as if he thought she was going to break.

Courtney turned to him, lowering her voice. "Why don't you let her play? All children like to run around. It's only natural."

His eyes darkened. Maybe for once she was trying to be nice, but that still didn't give her the right to butt in where she didn't belong. "How many children do you have?"

There they were again, on opposite sides. By now, she should be getting used to this. "She's my only one at the moment."

Oh no, not here, lady. You don't belong in this part of my life. "No, she's mine." His voice was low, even and would brook no argument. "I'll thank you to leave my daughter to me."

Courtney shoved her hands into her back pockets. All right, maybe she had been a little lofty, but he'd rubbed her the wrong way. "I don't see why—"

There was no arguing this point. But maybe she needed the rules spelled out to her.

"Look, you bought me for two years, you didn't buy Katie." Squatting, he rummaged through his toolbox, not really focusing on anything that was inside. "That means you have no say in the way I raise her." He wanted his daughter to have fun, to be happy, but he was so afraid of overtaxing her heart. "I shouldn't have even let you give her that dog." He knew why she'd done it, and had even been moved by her thoughtfulness. But maybe it had been a mistake to accept it.

Courtney curbed the urge to tell him what she thought of him. She knew it was pointless. He didn't care what she thought of him. But he did care about Katie. Didn't he like seeing her happy?

Courtney watched Katie playing with Squiggles. "They look like they belong together."

They did—or they would, after Katie was well. "Yeah, well, to your lawyer, so do we."

It was like arguing with a rock. She let the matter go. "I haven't thanked you for that yet. Standing still for Parsons's questions. The morning after my—our wedding," she reminded him when he looked at her blankly.

He'd rather enjoyed pretending to be the loving spouse. Especially since he could see that it made her nervous. Courtney had a little vein at the side of throat that throbbed whenever she was agitated. It had throbbed a great deal when he'd held her to him for the lawyer's benefit.

And maybe, he admitted, a little for his own.

John shrugged, finally zeroing in on the plane he was looking for. "Just doing my job."

That's all it was to him. A job. And she was paying him for it. Handsomely. There was no need to thank him, she upbraided herself ruefully. Her check would do that more than adequately.

"Well, your services are needed again, husband-for-hire," she informed him coldly. "I'm having a party Saturday—"

"Don't you people do anything except party?"

She clenched her hands at her sides, not wanting to lose her temper in front of Katie. "I wish you'd stop referring to me as 'you people.' In case you haven't noticed, I'm not a crowd, I'm an individual."

"Oh, I've noticed all right. Probably more than either one of us would want." That stopped her, he noted. He really didn't want to argue with her. It was just that whenever Courtney was around, he found himself getting testy.

PLAY
SILHOUETTE'S

LUCKY HEARTS
GAME

AND YOU GET

★ FREE BOOKS

★ A FREE GIFT

★ AND MUCH MORE

TURN THE PAGE AND
DEAL YOURSELF IN →

PLAY "LUCKY HEARTS" AND GET...

★ **Exciting Silhouette Special Edition® novels—FREE**

★ **PLUS a beautiful Cherub Magnet—FREE**

THEN CONTINUE YOUR LUCKY STREAK WITH A SWEETHEART OF A DEAL

1. Play Lucky Hearts as instructed on the opposite page.
2. Send back this card and you'll receive brand-new Silhouette Special Edition® novels. These books have a cover price of $3.99 each, but they are yours to keep absolutely free.
3. There's no catch. You're under no obligation to buy anything. We charge nothing — ZERO — for your first shipment. And you don't have to make any minimum number of purchases — not even one!
4. The fact is thousands of readers enjoy receiving books by mail from the Silhouette Reader Service. They like the convenience of home delivery...they like getting the best new novels months before they're available in stores...and they love our discount prices!
5. We hope that after receiving your free books you'll want to remain a subscriber. But the choice is yours — to continue or cancel, anytime at all! So why not take us up on our invitation, with no risk of any kind. You'll be glad you did!

And when she wasn't around, he found himself thinking about her. And getting testy.

Because he didn't want to want her as much as he did.

There was no one else around to take his frustration out on. So she got the brunt of it. It was only fitting, seeing how she was the cause of it.

"And what's that supposed to mean?" she demanded.

"You're a smart girl. You figure it out."

"It's not 'girl' these days," Courtney corrected him. "It's 'woman.'"

His eyes drifted over her body, remembering how she'd looked wearing that spiderweb she called a nightgown. "I've noticed that, too." He obviously wasn't going to get any work done with her lingering around him. John turned around to face her squarely, giving her his undivided attention. "Okay, what am I supposed to do at this party?"

"Behave." She saw his eyes narrowing and held up her hand. It had been a cheap shot and she knew it. "Truce. I'm just going to introduce you to some of the people who weren't at the wedding—"

He knew she'd said it was going to be part of the deal, but he didn't have to like it. The thought of being "introduced" to even more of her shallow friends rubbed a very raw, very familiar spot. "Are you going to parade me around on a leash, or do I get to roam free like a tame pet?"

She was getting tired of his balking at everything. "No one twisted your arm to agree to this bargain."

A mirthless smile creased his lips. "No, you're right, no one did. Sorry." He began planing the bottom of the door. When he had tested it earlier, it had stuck on the door sill. "I'll be there."

The about-face left her suspicious. "In a suit, this time."

He shrugged, applying muscle as he moved the plane along. "In anything you want."

Wood shavings fell at her feet. Courtney moved back. "You know, you really don't have to do that. After all, you're supposed to be my husband."

"Don't the husbands in your world have hobbies?" More shavings rained down. He tested the side of the door with his finger, then decided to give it one more pass. "Your father did. Besides, anyone you hire won't do as good a job as I can."

"Think a lot of yourself, don't you?"

He glanced and was surprised to see a smile on her face. He swallowed the retort that had risen to his lips. "Only when it's merited. Now, if you don't mind, you're in my way."

Well, politeness certainly wasn't his long suit, she thought. Courtney turned on her heel without saying a word.

Gabriel watched as she left. It was a hell of a predicament he'd gotten himself into.

But he'd survived Diane and he could survive this. Although, he had to admit that he didn't remember Diane ever affecting him quite like this.

He saw Katie hurrying after Courtney, struggling with the puppy she held in her arms. "Katie, where are you going?" he called after her.

"With Mommy," she cried.

Turning, Courtney saw Katie's slow progress. She crossed to her and took the puppy.

"Come here, Squiggles." Sloan was going to love this, she thought. "I'm going to have to ask Mandy how she toilet trained her dog."

"Don't you mean housebroke?" Katie offered her the word her father had used.

"No, I think Squiggles has got breaking things in the house pretty much down pat."

Katie giggled and Courtney slipped her free hand around the little girl's shoulders as they walked into the house.

Hell of a predicament, John thought again. It took him a few minutes before he got back to work.

Chapter Nine

Courtney didn't see them immediately. The carefully handmade card and the tiny rectangular box with its navy blue bow were sitting off to the side on the vanity table, out of her direct line of vision.

When Courtney first walked into the room out of the shower, her bathrobe wrapped around her, her mind was touching on a dozen last-minute details concerning the party that night. She wanted everything to be perfect.

An uncustomary flutter of nerves rushed over her. Exhaling, she ran her fingers through her hair. Already beginning to dry and curl, it felt like a mass of tangles to the touch.

Courtney glanced at the mirror, frowning. Should she leave it that way? Or wear it up? Gathering her hair off her neck, she examined the results. It didn't help make up her mind.

Gabriel would probably think all this was trivial. But

it wasn't. She was thirty today, and while that might not be earthshaking, it meant something to her. She wasn't just a carefree kid anymore. There were responsibilities awaiting her.

More responsibilities, she amended. It wasn't as if she'd been a madcap heiress up to now, although Gabriel probably thought so.

Gabriel.

Her frown deepened. Why did all her thoughts keep circling around him, returning to him as if he were some kind of mystical point of origin? Courtney picked up a comb and tried to pull it through her hair. Resistance met her. Just like Gabriel.

Was she making a mistake? She needed the party, the diversion it created, but she knew that Gabriel didn't like having to attend. Forcing him to mingle so soon with her friends might be putting too much pressure on him. To his credit, he'd borne up to the wedding and the interview with Parsons pretty well so far. It really wasn't fair of her to expect so much so quickly.

But the party was supposed to be in his honor. He couldn't very well not show up. If he was absent, rumors would start flying.

Rumors would probably start anyway, Courtney thought. She knew this crowd. A lot of them lived for rumors.

Courtney reached for her moisturizer. Her skin felt like leather lately. Or was that just tension constricting everything?

Her fingers came in contact with paper rather than the familiar round jar.

She looked down on the vanity and saw the card, and the gift sitting behind it. Curious, she picked them both up.

Who—?

There were three stick figures drawn on the front cover of the card. One was very obviously a man, and his pointy little hand was holding on to the equally pointy little hand of a smaller, blonder figure. They were both looking at a much larger figure, also blond, and if the less-than-artful shoes on the stick feet were any indication, this was a female.

Courtney's smile spread, filling her. No one had ever drawn a picture for her before. Certainly not *of* her. Above the figures, in childish scrawl, were the words *Happy Birthday, Mommy*.

She could feel her throat tightening as she read. Just a silly little piece of paper, she thought. A silly, little, dear piece of paper.

Inside the card, in lettering that was far more ornate than what was on the outside, were the words *Yeah, me, too*. Beneath was Gabriel's signature, followed by a drawing of a hammer and chisel.

She'd gotten a birthday card from Rambo and his child. Who knew that beneath that monosyllabic exterior beat the heart of an artist? Courtney blinked back a sudden tear and sat down on her bed, staring at the card. The gift lay clutched in her other hand, unopened and, for the time being, forgotten.

Holding the card brought back memories. Courtney could remember sitting and drawing a card for her father on his birthday. One of the servants had gently offered to take her to a store to buy one, saying that her father would prefer a real card. But she had stubbornly refused, finishing the one she was making. Her father had professed it to be his dearest treasure. Less than a year later, she'd thought he was just being kind.

She knew now that he hadn't been. He really had treasured the card. Just as she treasured this one.

Courtney glanced toward the connecting door. How had they known that her birthday was today?

There was only one way to find out. She slipped the wrapped box into the pocket of her bathrobe.

"Katie," she called, walking into the little girl's room.

Katie was already in bed. Gabriel was sitting beside her, an open storybook in his hands. Courtney saw that, unlike her, he was already dressed for the party. And he was wearing the suit that she'd laid out for him. She couldn't understand why he'd resisted wearing it before. The suit looked wonderful on him.

Sackcloth and ashes would have looked wonderful on him, she thought, remembering what she'd said about dressing for an interrogation.

Katie sat up, the sleepy look fading from her eyes as she saw the card in Courtney's hand. Squiggles, lying asleep at the foot of the bed, raised his head, then went back to sleep.

"You found it. I told Daddy I didn't think you saw the card I drewed—"

"Drew," John corrected automatically. How could an ordinary bathrobe look so damn enticing? But it did. On her. Especially the small area that was still wet, just across her breasts. He wondered if he had enough time to take a cold shower.

"—Drew for you," Katie continued. She looked at Courtney eagerly, eyes shining. "Do you like it?"

Courtney pressed the card to her heart. "It's the most beautiful card I've ever received."

And it was, because there was love in every stroke. At least on the front, she amended. She wondered how

Katie had managed to convince Gabriel to write something on the inside. The little girl obviously had hidden talents that bore looking into.

Courtney sat down on the edge of the bed. "How did you know?"

Katie turning, pointing to her father. "Daddy told me."

"Daddy?" Courtney looked at Gabriel. She wouldn't have thought that he'd trouble himself to find out when her birthday was. "How did you—?"

John shrugged, feeling uncomfortable with the attention focused on his actions. "Mandy thought I should know."

Mandy would. She could only guess what her best friend had said to him to get Gabriel to do this. Courtney flushed, feeling the need to apologize for Mandy. "You didn't have to feel obligated to get me something."

"I didn't feel obligated," he replied mildly.

If it had been presented as an obligation, he wouldn't have done anything. But Mandy had painted a very convincing scene of a poor little rich girl and he'd had to admit that it had aroused his sympathies somewhat. He knew what it felt like to have your birthday overlooked. He'd spent most of his childhood that way, not really meaning enough to anyone for them to remember a day he had once thought was special.

John nodded toward the door. "Don't you think you should be getting ready?"

As Courtney slipped her hand into her pocket, her fingers touched her gift. She took the box out and just looked at it. A card, and a gift, too. Just when she thought she had him figured out...

"Everyone always expects me to be late."

His discomfort was growing in direct proportion to

the emotion he detected in her voice. "Why don't you surprise them?"

Katie scrambled forward. "Aren't you going to open it?" Katie urged. She'd helped her father pick out the gift. It made her feel very important to be involved in such a grown-up decision. Her eyes eagerly anticipated Courtney's reaction. "It's beautiful," she whispered solemnly.

Courtney held the box a moment longer, savoring the feel of it. He'd actually bought her a gift, she thought. After she'd said all those things to him. A more cynical person might have thought that he was just trying to win her over, but she knew there was no reason for him to. And something told her that he wasn't like that.

"It's nothing." When he'd bought the gift, he'd been attracted to its simplicity. Now he wondered what the hell he'd been thinking. It wouldn't be anything more than a trinket for her. She'd probably laugh at it.

Very carefully, Courtney removed the bow and then opened the velvet box. There, resting on an insert as black as the inside of midnight, was a thin gold braided chain.

It was stupid of him to feel this nervous. "You probably have a dozen like them," he muttered, shoving his hands in his pockets.

She raised her eyes to his. Why had she thought she knew anything about this man? He was far too complex to be summarily dismissed with the few simple words she'd affixed to him.

"No, I don't," she whispered.

He blew out a breath, annoyed with himself for ever having gone out of his way. All he'd managed to do was make a fool of himself. There had been enough of that years ago. "Right, yours are all thicker and more expensive."

"Will you stop?" The order was issued softly.

Courtney swallowed the lump that had suddenly formed. She could have bought herself anything she wanted to. But she couldn't have bought herself this, for it came wrapped in feelings of inordinate sweetness. Sweetness that filled her heart and her very soul.

She bit her lip and looked at Katie, then up at Gabriel. "I don't really know what to say."

He wished she'd just hand him the damn thing and let him take it back. "'Receipt, please,' comes to mind."

This time, she wasn't going to let sarcasm drive a space between them. Not when she was holding something precious in her hands. "Why?"

Avoiding the puzzled look in Katie's eyes, he gestured at the box disparagingly. "So you can take it back."

"I don't want to take it back," she insisted. She ran her hand along Katie's hair. Katie curled into her touch. "I want to wear it."

Why was she lying? The cheapest thing in her jewelry box probably cost three times as much as the chain in her hand. "No, you don't."

Courtney dropped her hand from Katie's head and looked at him. Why was he finding her gratitude so hard to accept?

"Don't tell me what I want, Gabriel." She raised herself on her toes, the heat of her words giving way to another sort of heat. The one she felt whenever she was so close to him. It seemed that no matter what she did, however much she tried to keep some distance between them, the very real, very strong attraction she felt just kept on growing. It was just a matter of time before it swallowed her up.

Just a matter of time before she gave in to it.

"You haven't got a clue what's on my mind now."

He looked at her and saw something in her eyes. Something that mirrored what he was feeling. "Yeah," he answered quietly, "maybe I do."

The pregnant moment had nowhere to go. There was a child in the room. Courtney offered the box to him. "Put it on for me?"

Not waiting for an answer, she turned her back on him and then slipped her robe off her shoulders. Taking her hair in one hand, she moved it off her neck, giving him a clear field.

He wanted to press his lips to the slim column she'd exposed. To kiss her until the robe slipped down to her toes...

He pulled a ragged breath back into his lungs and removed the chain from the box. With hands that were suddenly clumsy, it took him a few minutes before he managed to secure the catch at the base of her neck. Finished, he stepped back, his hands raised in the air as if he were afraid that one more moment of contact would make him not responsible for his actions.

She turned around to face him, the thin Florentine chain gleaming at her throat. "It's beautiful," she told him.

Yes it was, he thought. But she was the one who made it beautiful.

He cleared his throat, finally finding his voice. "Mandy said you didn't want anyone giving you anything, that you didn't want them remembering it was your birthday." His expression said that he didn't believe that. "Everyone should have their birthday remembered."

Because looking at the expression on Courtney's face

was messing with his mind, he turned away. He liked it better when she was angry at him.

She wouldn't have guessed that he was the sentimental type. But then, he hadn't struck her as particularly thoughtful, either. There was just so much she didn't know about him. Beginning with his birthday.

"I don't know when yours is."

"May fourth," he finally answered.

"I'll remember it," Courtney promised, her voice thick with emotion.

"Mine's September fifteenth," Katie piped up.

For a moment, she'd almost forgotten the little girl was in the room. Courtney smiled at her now, hugging Katie to her. "And we'll have a huge party for you," she promised, envisioning it. Her father used to throw the best birthday parties for her. "With clowns—"

John saw the look on Katie's face. He knew how she felt, and knew that she was too polite to say anything. "Clowns scare her."

"No clowns," Courtney decreed instantly. She raised her brows questioningly. "Ponies?"

Katie clapped her hands together. Seeing her warmed John's heart. And without his consciously realizing it, his daughter's joy caused his heart to open for Courtney.

"I love ponies," Katie exclaimed. Her father had never let her sit on one, but she had lots of books with pictures of ponies in them and it was her dream to ride one someday.

"Then ponies it is," Courtney promised, delighted to have found something that pleased Katie. "Lots of ponies."

"We'll see," John told his daughter. After the operation, there would be time enough to make plans for activities that would no longer tax her. For now, he didn't want Katie getting too excited.

There was something here, Courtney thought, something she didn't quite understand. But she intended to get to the bottom of it...eventually.

She ran her hand along the necklace. ''Well, I'd better go get ready.'' She looked at John and smiled. ''Might as well surprise everyone for a change.''

He nodded. ''Might as well.''

No, he was definitely not an easy man to understand, Courtney thought, slipping out of the room.

''Do you like her better now, Daddy?'' she heard Katie ask just as she'd reached the hall.

What she couldn't hear was his reply. He'd shut the door before answering.

Her fingers skimmed along the necklace and Courtney smiled to herself. Maybe she had had a glimpse of the answer, anyway.

She shouldn't have done this, Courtney thought, making her way across the crowded room. She shouldn't have had this party so soon on the heels of the wedding reception. Thinking about it now, she didn't know what had possessed her. She didn't need to introduce John to everyone. Word of mouth would have spread quickly enough.

She looked over toward him now, feeling anxious. Like a mother hen, she thought, mocking herself. As if he needed her worrying about him. He'd probably resent it if he knew. John was blending in smoothly enough. The women around him saw to that.

But she could tell he was uncomfortable.

Funny how she'd become tuned in to his feelings all

of a sudden, she mused. For now, she pushed the thought aside, not wanting to explore it.

Courtney managed to catch John's eye before she reached him. She was too far away for him to hear her, so she nodded toward the patio. He looked relieved as he extricated himself from the group around him. All women, she noted.

John opened the door for her just as she reached him. The night air had a soothing chill to it. She let it wrap itself around her before she looked at John. "How are you holding up?"

He was surprised that she even asked. Leaning against the railing, he stared out into the darkness. A single silvery stream of moonlight cut through it. A symphony of crickets serenaded them. Their music rivaled the expensive band playing inside.

"I've been better. Kind of reminds me of old times." He looked at her. "My ex loved parties. Insisted I be there to endure her friends' scrutiny." He looked away. He was talking too much, he thought. For some reason, he continued. "At least, in the beginning. After a while, she liked it better when I stayed away."

Courtney tried to put herself in his shoes, to see her friends through his eyes. How would it feel, being the outsider, knowing that everyone was looking at you, evaluating you? She almost shivered. "They're not scrutinizing you."

She wasn't being defensive, she was trying to make him feel better, he realized. "Aren't they?"

He wasn't the type to be lied to, or to find comfort in lies. "All right," she relented. "Maybe they are. But it's nothing personal. They scrutinize everyone." Courtney thought about it, about the people she had known for most of her life. "I guess, maybe that's their insecurity coming through.'' She turned, leaning back against the railing, looking at him. He looked so rugged against the moonlight. She had to remind herself to breathe. ''Being rich has its own set of rules, its own problems.''

As soon as it was out of her mouth, Courtney realized how self-serving that must have sounded to him. She wouldn't have been surprised if he laughed at the sentiments.

But he didn't. ''Yeah, I know.''

He sounded as if he was serious. As if he really knew the inside of this world he was visiting. She tried to make some sense out of it. ''You don't think money can cure everything?'

John laughed softly, but there was little humor in the sound. ''I was there. I know it can't. It can't make you happy, that's for sure.'' His ex-in-laws were living proof of that. He sincerely doubted that between them they had known a happy day their entire lives.

Courtney didn't understand. ''Then why are you doing this?''

For a moment, he debated telling her. But that, he thought, was only the champagne and the moonlight clouding his mind. Common sense had taught him to keep his own counsel. That way, the facts couldn't be twisted and used against him somehow.

''It can't buy you happiness,'' he allowed, ''but it can buy you peace of mind.''

Could it? she wondered. Could it buy his? What sort of a price tag was attached to his peace of mind? ''And what would it take to buy your peace of mind?''

He wasn't about to tell her that, or to take the discussion any further than it had already gone. He'd said too much as it was, talked more than he had in years, even to his old college buddy, Rick.

John touched her chain with the tip of his finger. He watched her eyes flutter as he lightly skimmed the hollow of her throat. A look came over her face, a look etched in desire. He felt something tightening within him. A spring that was going to have to be released soon, before it exploded.

"You really don't have to wear that, you know. You won't hurt my feelings." He grinned. "I've got a tough hide."

She laughed. "Tell me about it." They hadn't moved any closer, yet the space between them seemed to be shrinking. "And as for 'have to,' I think you'll learn that I never do what I have to."

It might be what she chose to believe, but it wasn't true. "You married me."

Her eyes met his, whispering things that she couldn't say out loud. Things Courtney wasn't quite ready to admit to just yet, even to herself. But the thoughts were there, just the same. Waiting until she could unwrap them without fear.

"Yes, I did."

Drawn to the softness he heard in her voice, John cupped his hand along her cheek and turned her face up to his. Lightly, he touched his lips to hers, then backed away, knowing it wasn't safe to do anything else. Not yet, not when his own emotions were so scrambled.

There was surprise in her eyes, and wonder. He smiled. "Happy birthday, Courtney."

It was one of the few times he'd actually said her name. And the first without sarcasm or defiance. She could feel her heart swelling. Part of her silently screamed, *No!* because she knew what would happen if she let go, if she allowed herself to feel.

And what would happen afterward.

But a tiny bit of her mourned. Mourned because she wanted it to happen so very badly. More than anything, she wanted to taste that heady feeling of falling in love again, of pretending that, this time, it had a prayer of actually working out.

Maybe she still did believe in fairy tales.

Courtney nodded toward the doors. "We'd better go back in," she murmured.

He wasn't going to argue. There was something about standing with her in the moonlight that sapped away his resolve, making him forget a past that should have taught him a lesson.

Reaching for the door, he opened it, letting her walk in first. As they entered, they overheard a fragment of a conversation. It took Courtney only a second to realize that they weren't meant to overhear.

"Well, where do you think she found him?" Kimberly Weston asked the man at her side.

Harrison Chandler, the latest of Kimberly's lovers, finished his glass of wine and picked another off a tray before asking, "Where?"

"In her own backyard." Kimberly's laugh sounded as if she'd spent time rehearsing the melodic sound to achieve just the right timbre. "The best that money can buy, so I hear."

Harrison had been sniffing around Courtney's boots not more than six months ago. Courtney clenched the hands at her sides into fists.

"Really?" Harrison's laugh had a nasty edge to it. "I would have thought if she was in the market, she could have done a lot better."

Like you? Courtney thought.

His mouth curved wickedly. "Someone said he was a carpenter."

John took Courtney's arm. He didn't need to hear any more of this. He was surprised when she pulled her arm away angrily.

Rather than walk away, she thrust herself between Kimberly and Harrison. The latter almost dropped his drink. He had the good grace to look chagrined. Kimberly chose to brazen it out, meeting Courtney's glare with a show of innocence.

"He's an engineer. Carpentry is his hobby." Courtney's eyes narrowed as she remembered Harrison's clumsy attempts to seduce her. "And you're not fit to clean his shoes, Harry."

Kimberly laid a hand on Harrison's arm. "Oh, Courtney, darling. I didn't realize you were there."

"Obviously, 'darling.'" Courtney turned to John. "Let's go, John." Before he could respond, she took his hand. "The air suddenly smells of something sour." With that, she turned away, all but burrowing through the crowd.

"Hold on." John turned her around before Courtney had the opportunity to plow across half the floor. "This isn't a race."

She had gotten them to the dance floor without realizing it. The band was playing a slow song. He did what came all too naturally to him. He took her into his arms.

Swaying, she followed his lead without being completely aware of what she was doing. She was so angry at Kimberly and Harrison she could scream. And angry at herself for inadvertently subjecting John to their mean-spirited drivel. He deserved better than to hear himself picked apart like that.

"I just wanted to get away before I hit her." She bristled a little at the amused look on his face, then forced herself to simmer down. "I wouldn't have regretted it, of course, but I would have ruined a perfectly good manicure.''

He couldn't help laughing. "I've never had anyone defend me before. Do you know your eyes blaze when you're angry? I thought that emotion was strictly reserved for me."

She hadn't been fair to him, she thought ruefully. "What, you think you're the only one who gets me angry?" She shook her head. "Money isn't the only thing my father willed to me. He gave me his temper, too." She sighed, looking over her shoulder toward where Kimberly and Harrison had stood. They were gone now. Good. "My father never could stomach a snob."

John pressed her hand to his chest, covering it. He liked the feel of her heart near his. This was getting dangerous, he realized.

"Then why do you invite them to your parties?"

She gave him an honest answer. "They have money—I have a pet charity. They like to look important, so they write huge checks." Her gaze took in half the floor. There were a lot of good people here. There was no reason to lump them in with the likes of Kimberly and Harrison just because they had money. "Besides, not everyone's like that. A lot of them are pretty nice."

He nodded. "Like Mandy."

It wasn't a question. He was telling her. "Like Mandy." She raised her head to look at him. "Do you?" Courtney asked, then, when he didn't answer, added, "Like Mandy?"

He didn't have to think about his answer. "Yes, I do. She seems pretty nice. And she tipped me off about your birthday." That was something only a friend would do, John thought. "I think she expected me to get you something."

Then he *had* gotten the gift out of a sense of obligation. Suddenly she could feel the outline of the chain as it rested against her throat. It felt heavier. "You didn't have to."

He thought they'd settled that. "You want me to tell you that I wanted to? All right, I wanted to." He avoided her eyes as he made the admission.

"Why?" She hadn't exactly been the model of friendliness toward him.

He laughed shortly, moving her slowly in time to the music. He saw the envy in men's eyes as they looked in his direction. It made no difference to him. Envy wasn't something that affected him one way or the other.

"Boy, you don't ask for much, do you? How much of my guts do you want me to spill out?"

The question had her smiling in response. "I'll let you know."

No, he'd told her as much as he was going to. "Not tonight, Ms. Tamberlaine."

She caught her lower lip between her teeth, then asked, "Say it again."

"Tamberlaine." Why would she want to hear that?

"No, my first name. Say my first name."

"Why, did you forget it?" His smile was soft, sexy. "Courtney," he repeated.

"Thank you." Leaning her cheek against his chest, Courtney closed her eyes and let the music take her away.

Maybe turning thirty wasn't so bad, after all.

Chapter Ten

"Were there lots of pretty people at the party?" Katie looked from one side of the dining room table to the other, waiting for an answer.

Courtney took another sip of her black coffee. The caffeine was taking an inordinately long time to kick in. But then, maybe at seven-thirty, *it* was half-asleep, too. She'd felt more wide-awake at seven when her eyes had suddenly flown open. She wasn't sure just what had woken her up, but the second her eyes were open, her thoughts had immediately focused on last night. On John. Once she began thinking of the way his body had felt against hers when they'd danced, she became far too restless to remain in bed.

It had been worth getting up at this ungodly hour just to see the look of surprise on John's face when he came downstairs and found her already in the dining room.

"Lots of pretty people, pumpkin," she answered.

Katie was doing justice to the big breakfast in front
of her. She obviously got her appetite from her father,
who was on his second serving of pancakes. Courtney's
stomach tightened at the mere thought of food. For as
long as she could remember, she'd never been able to
face anything solid until at least noon.

"Depends on your definition of pretty," John murmured, more to himself than to his daughter.

Katie didn't seem to hear him. She was completely
focused on what Courtney was saying. Swallowing what
was in her mouth, she enthused, "Ohh, I wish I could've
been there."

She sounded like Cinderella, wishing she could have
attended the ball. Courtney could remember a time when
she had thought of the people at her father's parties in
the same light.

Now she was a little more realistic.

But if Cinderella wanted a peek into the ballroom,
Cinderella was going to get a peek. "Maybe next time
I'll let you stay up for a little while and you can see for
yourself," Courtney promised.

Katie looked as if she was in heaven.

The expression on John's face brought a different lo-
cation to mind. Obviously, he thought she was usurping
his authority. After last night, Courtney had thought that
they were past this stage.

Progress, it seemed, was a slow thing.

Katie turned her bright eyes on her father. "Can I,
Daddy? Can I? Can I stay up and see everyone next
time?"

With any luck, the "next time" would be far in the
future. He certainly didn't want Katie losing sleep just
to see a room full of people who didn't have anything

better to do than throw money away on overpriced clothing.

He gave Katie his usual noncommittal, "We'll see."
The vague response didn't seem to dampen her spirits,
but it did grate on Courtney's nerves.

There was love in Katie's eyes as she looked at Courtney. Love in the purest state possible. Forgetting about
being annoyed at John, Courtney gave Katie her full
attention. She was at a loss as to how she merited being
the recipient of something so precious.

As John looked at his daughter's beaming face, he was
sincerely doubting the wisdom of his actions. He should
have never brought Katie here.

"I bet Mommy was the prettiest one there. Wasn't
she, Daddy?"

John pushed his plate aside. He raised his eyes to
Courtney's face, remembering the way she had looked
on the terrace, the moonlight shining along her skin. It
was enough to make a man's mouth water.

He'd never lied to Katie. He wasn't going to start
now. "Yes, she was."

His tone was low, as if it were coming from somewhere deep within him. It unsettled Courtney. If she
didn't know better, she would have thought John was
actually paying her a compliment instead of just humor-
ing his daughter.

She took a deep breath to steady the quiver in the pit
of her stomach, then raised her cup to her lips to hide
her pleased smile. But her eyes gave her away. "Thank
you."

Katie suddenly twisted around in her chair, her entire
body animated as she faced her father. "Can Mommy
come with us?"

The request disappointed him. He'd wanted Katie to

himself today. For the past two weeks, they had been on the estate. Though it was large, there was always some lingering reminder of Courtney to haunt him no matter where he went. And then, like as not, there was the lady herself to deal with. Today it was just supposed to be the two of them. He'd expected to be gone by the time Courtney was up. After last night, he felt certain she was going to sleep in past noon.

The woman never did what was expected of her.

John moved aside as the maid, Angela, came out of the kitchen to clear away his plate. Having someone else wait on him always made him uncomfortable. It was something he was never going to get used to.

Looking at Katie, he hedged. "Well, I don't know. Courtney—Mommy," he corrected himself for Katie's benefit, "probably has other plans." At least he fervently hoped so.

What were they up to? Courtney wondered. She'd promised to get together with Mandy today, but Mandy was flexible, especially since she was currently between men now that Louis and his private jet had been unceremoniously dumped. They could reschedule. And this was far more promising.

Courtney leaned her head on her upturned palm, looking straight into Katie's eyes. John's were too dark for her to risk just yet. "Actually, I don't have plans. Where are you going?"

"To the 'musement park." She leaned her chin on her palm, mimicking Courtney to a T. "Disneyland." She said the name as if it was synonymous with heaven.

"Today?" Courtney raised her brow toward John. This was the first she'd heard about it.

"Today," John echoed quickly. "So if you're busy, we understand—"

"No, I'm not. Really," she insisted. Why did he refuse to believe her? Or was it that he was just subtly refusing to let her come along? "When did you plan this?"

He shrugged her question off. "It's just a last-minute thing."

It wasn't Katie he was lying to, he told himself. It was Courtney. He'd made the decision to take Katie to the amusement park at the beginning of the week. Right after he'd gotten off the telephone with her cardiologist. Dr. Benjamin had told him that there was a spot open at the end of the month for Katie's surgery. The doctor wanted the go-ahead in order to put together the necessary surgical teams and reserve an operating room for that day. The surgery promised to be a long one.

After less than a moment's soul-searching, John had given his okay.

The pieces were all coming together and he was scared as hell. He wanted to give Katie as good a time as he could before she had to go in to face the bypass-surgery.

It wasn't that he wouldn't get another opportunity, he insisted fiercely. It was just that it would take Katie a while to bounce back from the surgery. And then there would be school to face. He'd learned a long time ago not to put things off. This just fell under that heading, that's all.

He was lying to her, Courtney thought. She didn't know why, but he was. She could see it in his eyes.

Why would he lie about something so insignificant as planning a trip to Disneyland with his daughter?

She was beginning to think she was never going to understand him. But then, she didn't have to. He'd be gone out of her life soon enough. And besides, all that really mattered right now was the little girl sitting opposite her.

Courtney covered Katie's hand with her own. "Well, I'm glad you asked me because I would love nothing better than to come along."

Why? Why would a woman who could be anywhere in the world she chose to be want to spend her day at an amusement park with a little girl and her father? It didn't make any sense to him. She'd be bored to tears inside of thirty minutes. Less.

"The park opens at nine today," he told Courtney, hoping for one last way out. "I'd like to be there when it opens. The lines are shorter then and Katie'll have a chance to go on more of the rides."

Courtney was already on her feet. She glanced at her watch. It was only a few minutes past eight. Barring a traffic jam, they were only thirty minutes away from the Magic Kingdom. "Just give me ten minutes to get ready."

Famous last words, John thought as he watched her leave. He'd give her the ten minutes, no more. After that, he was gone. He and Katie had better things to do than cool their heels while Courtney tried to find an outfit that pleased her.

She didn't take ten minutes. She took nine, completely surprising him. He was sitting on the bottom step when she came flying down the stairs in sandals, shorts and a halter top. Her bare leg brushed against his arm, sending currents through both of them that had nothing to do with the warm day that was beginning to unfold outside.

Rising to his feet, he saw that her skin glowed with suntan lotion and enthusiasm. She was breathless—and breathtakingly simple. With her hair pulled back from her face in an ordinary ponytail, she almost looked like a teenager. And very much the way he envisioned Katie would look when she reached her teens.

"No makeup," John noted out loud before he thought better of it.

She smiled. "Mickey doesn't like it." Courtney took Katie's hand. "See, I said I'd be ready in ten minutes."

He had to give her her due. "You made it with a minute to spare."

There was triumph and laughter in her eyes. It was an appealing combination. "I knew you were timing me. And that you wouldn't wait."

Katie shook her head. She didn't even have to look at her father to back her up. "We'd always wait for you, Mommy."

Yeah, right, Courtney thought, glancing at John. At breakfast he'd looked as if he couldn't wait to get away from her. She grinned, ruffling Katie's hair. "Thanks, pumpkin. Okay, Disneyland, here we come."

Katie cheered as they walked out.

"You know," Courtney mused out loud as she plucked at the cotton candy cone in her hand. A tuft of pink spun sugar came off in her fingers. "This was my very favorite place in the world as a kid. My dad used to bring me here all the time." She popped the tuft into her mouth and smiled as it melted away on her tongue.

Sitting beside her on the bench, John helped himself to some of Courtney's cotton candy. He hadn't wanted a cone of his own, but she made it look so appealing, he couldn't resist sampling a taste. "I'm surprised he didn't buy it for you."

If there was a touch of sarcasm in his voice, she chose to overlook it. John had bought himself a lot of grace with that gift of his, she thought fondly. Besides, she was feeling very magnanimous this afternoon. And very, very good.

"He rented it for me once," she admitted. Another piece of the pink cloud disappeared on her tongue. She offered some of the remainder to John. Katie had her own cone and had made short work of it. "For my tenth birthday."

Katie looked at her as if she had suddenly become magical. It was clear that she was imagining having her own birthday party at Disneyland. "Did they all come? Mickey and Donald and Cinderella?"

Courtney nodded. "All of them." Along with a whole crowd of her friends, as well as her father's friends and their children. She'd felt like a princess in a fairy tale that day. Suddenly, Courtney wanted very much to give Katie that same special feeling. "Would you like that, pumpkin? Would you like to have a birthday party here?"

It was just too wonderful to think about. "Instead of the ponies?"

Courtney laughed. It was obvious that ponies meant a lot to Katie. "With the ponies. We'll find a way to get them all tickets, too, if you like."

This was getting way out of hand, John thought. And they were all just empty promises. People in the world Courtney came from had a habit of forgetting promises. He knew that firsthand and he didn't want Katie disappointed.

"We'll talk about it later, Katie. Right now, why don't you just enjoy the day?"

Gabriel was doing it again, Courtney thought, annoyed. Popping all the balloons. Why was he always so bent on dampening Katie's enthusiasm? He seemed to be against everything. The puppy, the promise of a party, the—

Courtney looked at him, stunned. Suddenly, the answer was crystal clear to her.

She was staring at him as if she'd just discovered he was a mass murderer. "What?"

She didn't answer him right away. "Katie, would you be a sweetheart and get me a soda?" Courtney pointed to the man standing behind the soft-drink cart. It was less than five feet away from the bench they were sitting on. "I'm very thirsty." She took out a five-dollar bill from her pocket and handed it to Katie.

John rose. He didn't want Katie running around by herself. "I'll get it."

Courtney placed her hand on his arm. It was a deceptively small hand with a firm grip. "No, I think it'll taste better if Katie gets it for me. She's a big girl now." She looked at her. "Aren't you, pumpkin?"

Katie seemed to grow an inch before their eyes as she raised her little chin importantly. "Yes, I am."

The bill clutched in her hand, Katie ran off to buy the soda for Courtney before her father could tell her not to.

Only when she thought that Katie was out of earshot did Courtney turn to him. "It's me, isn't it?"

He spared her a sharp glance before turning to watch his daughter. Maybe he was being a little overprotective, but it came with the territory. A direct result of almost losing her twice.

"What are you talking about?" he asked curtly. She had no business stirring Katie up like this.

"Every time I try to do something nice for Katie, you always try to negate it."

He still didn't have any idea what she was driving at. "That's ridiculous."

He wasn't very convincing. "Is it? I gave her the puppy...you told me you wished I hadn't. You keep telling her not to run around with him. I offer to throw her a party...you tell her 'we'll see' instead of getting high on the happiness shining in her eyes. I tell her she can stay up for our next party...you're there, saying no with every fiber of your being. Every time I try to do something, you don't want her to have any part of it.

"John, I'm not trying to take her away from you. I just want her to be happy."

His eyes were dark and dangerous as he looked into hers. "So do I."

She knew that, but she also knew he was doing it all wrong. He was clipping Katie's wings instead of letting her learn how to fly. That couldn't be good. For either of them. "So let her live a little."

"I am." The retort came out a little more fiercely than he'd intended, but she didn't know what she was talking about. "That's exactly what I am doing."

Again, Courtney had the eerie sense of something being kept from her. Something important. Damn it, why didn't he tell her instead of playing these secretive games?

"There's something you're not telling me, isn't there?"

John opened his mouth, then shut it again. He wasn't going to allow a moment of weakness to lead him. He'd come this far alone and he intended to make it the rest of the way.

"There are a lot of things I'm not telling you." He looked at her significantly. "Mainly because I'm too polite. But for the record, it's not you I'm reacting to. At least, not when it comes to things concerning Katie."

She could feel that wave again, the warm one that

wrapped itself around her tightly. "And when it comes to other things?"

He didn't answer her. Talking about it wouldn't help. It would only bring too much attention to feelings that were best left dormant.

Feelings, he knew, that weren't really dormant any longer.

Suddenly Katie returned, struggling to hold aloft a giant cup filled to the brim with soda.

"Here it is," Katie said proudly. "And I even have change." Since both her hands were filled with the cup, she could only indicate the money in her pocket with the point of her chin.

Courtney took the cup from her. "Keep it."

Katie's hand stopped midway into her pocket. She stared at Courtney. "Keep it? Really?"

Courtney nodded. "I think it's about time you started having an allowance." She shifted her eyes to John. "Right, Daddy?"

He was going to say that Katie was too young to handle money. But then he thought about it again. In every other way, Katie had displayed that she was far older than her years. Far more responsible that the average four-year-old. Why not in this area, too?

Maybe Courtney was partially right. Maybe he did feel as if he was being pushed to one side, his own light dimmed in the shadow of the aura she cast on his daughter. It was only natural to feel a little put out after being both mother and father to her for the past three and a half years.

Four, he corrected himself. Diane hadn't been there for her even in the beginning.

Well, whatever the psychological underpinnings, he

wasn't about to engage in a tug-of-war, not when the rope was his daughter.

Besides, he never could resist the eager look on Katie's face. "Right."

"Oh, boy. I like living with Mommy, Daddy."

He couldn't help laughing. "You would."

John rose, dusting off his hands. His fingertips still felt a little sticky from the cotton candy he'd stolen from Courtney. Everything, he mused, had consequences.

Behind him, he heard music coming from the giant carousel. They hadn't hit that ride yet, and now that the park was getting crowded, it was one of the few rides they wouldn't have to wait for an hour or more to get on.

"Anyone for the merry-go-round?" He pretended to look everywhere but at Katie.

Her hand shot up, waving to and fro in the sultry air. "Me, me."

Stooping, he presented his arm to her. "Then, your pony awaits, madam."

Katie giggled as she wrapped her arm around his. She looked over her shoulder at Courtney. "You, too, Mommy, right?"

"Me, too," Courtney promised. She had to walk slowly not to get ahead of them.

"We could have stayed for the fireworks," Courtney said with a touch of wistfulness as she tapped out the security code on the keypad. A bag filled to overflowing with souvenirs she'd bought for Katie was leaning haphazardly against the wall. With the alarm disarmed, she picked up the bag again and opened the door.

Or we could start some of our own. The thought, unbidden, came to her as she waited for him to walk in.

John had his own arms full. He was carrying Katie, who was sound asleep, her head nestled against him.

Careful not to wake her, he made his way slowly up the stairs. "I don't think even fireworks could pry her eyes open. She's exhausted." Maybe they'd overdone it, he thought guiltily. He should have brought Katie home hours ago. It was just that she was having so much fun, he didn't want it to end for her.

Ever.

With effort, he shut out the feeling that followed on the heels of that thought. If he started thinking along those lines, he wasn't going to be able to let her go through with the surgery. And then he'd lose her for sure.

Either way he turned, there was a sword pointed at his heart. He shook his head. To think he'd once yearned to grow up and be on his own.

But that was only because living under someone else's roof had been so intolerable. So what was he doing now? Now that he was so grown up? He was living under someone else's roof again.

It was different this time, he insisted silently. This was only temporary, a bargain, with a finite time involved, and then he could return to his own house. It wasn't like when he was living with his aunt and uncle. It wasn't even like when he was married to Diane, living in the house her parents insisted on buying for them. For *her,* he amended. Nothing had ever been done with him in mind. He'd just been the interloper.

Just as he was here, he reminded himself.

Following up the stairs behind him, Courtney watched Katie's sleeping face. She'd never thought very much about having children before. Never thought about it at all, actually. She'd been too much of a child herself, she supposed. Willful and wanting to be indulged.

She didn't feel like that now. She felt...maternal, she realized. It was a very odd, very sweet sensation.

Courtney bit her lip as she pushed the hair out of Katie's face. Maternal feelings somehow equated to worrying. The little girl seemed to tire awfully quickly, she thought, concern nibbling at her. She remembered having energy to spare at Katie's age.

It was probably just all the excitement and all the sugar she'd ingested, Courtney rationalized.

She walked ahead of John and opened the door to Katie's room.

"I'll get her ready for bed," Courtney volunteered. "Why don't you go downstairs and relax?" She moved to take the sleeping burden from him, but he held on to his daughter, walking over to the bed.

"I am relaxing," he answered. "Taking care of Katie isn't a chore for me." He laid her down on the bed. She murmured something in her sleep, then rolled over to her side. "I've been doing it since she was born."

One of Courtney's earliest memories was the scent of her mother's perfume as she hovered over her bed. "Your wife didn't put her to bed?"

He remembered the disdain on Diane's face. The complete absence of love in her eyes. "She didn't stay around long enough to get the hang of it. Besides, she never liked getting her hands dirty." He shrugged, not wanting to go into it.

Opening the top drawer in the bureau, he took out Katie's pajamas. When he turned around, he saw that Courtney had taken off Katie's sneakers and was working her socks off. "She hired a nanny to take care of things, but I didn't want Katie to see only strangers peering over her crib.''

There had been a squadron of doctors and nurses attending his daughter the first few months after her birth, helping her hang on to the thin thread that was all that tethered her to life.

Though he was immensely grateful to all of them, once Katie was home, he wanted his daughter to know that there was someone who loved her within call. Someone she could always depend on.

One nanny could hardly be called a crowd, Courtney thought, but she decided not to raise the point. She didn't want to argue with him, not tonight. All in all, it had been a really nice day. One of the best she'd had in recent memory.

Savoring the feeling, Courtney backed away, leaving him alone with his daughter. "All right, I'll be downstairs if you need me. I mean…''

"I know what you mean," he answered without turning around.

Maybe he did, she thought as she left the room, but *she* didn't. Things weren't so black-and-white to her anymore.

Chapter Eleven

"How was Disneyland, Madam?" Sloan asked Courtney when she walked into the living room.

For a moment, lost in thought, she'd forgotten that there was anyone else in the house besides the two people she had left upstairs. "It brought back memories, Sloan. A great many of them."

"All pleasant ones, I trust."

The smile on her face answered his question before she did. "Very pleasant."

Courtney was tired, as tired as Katie had seemed, but at the same time she felt too keyed up to sit. Crossing to the window, she pulled back the drape. The moonlight moved along the lawn, wrapping everything in dark velvet. She let the peaceful scene play upon her senses.

"Will you be requiring anything further, Madam?"

"Yes." Courtney stroked the drape's soft nap before turning from the window. "Could you find it in your heart not to call me madam? It really makes me feel like I'm a thousand years old."

He inclined his head, silently giving his word. "No one would mistake you for a thousand, mad—" Sloan paused. "What shall I call you? Mrs. Gabriel?" he suggested.

She wouldn't be Mrs. Gabriel for very long and there was a danger in becoming accustomed to hearing herself referred to that way. "Why don't you just keep on calling me Miss Courtney?" That would make the transition much smoother for the butler after John left.

But who was going to make the transition smoother for her?

Less than a month into the bargain and she was already getting very, very used to the idea of having him around. This hadn't been in her plans.

It was the chain, she thought. When John had given her the chain, her feelings, already in flux, had changed. Katie had softened her up.

The duo packed some one-two punch, she mused, running her fingers over the chain meditatively.

"Very good, Miss Courtney. Will you be wanting anything from the kitchen tonight?"

It was obvious he had somewhere else to go. The thought made her smile. She'd never thought about Sloan having a life outside these walls. But that was silly. Everyone did. It had just never occurred to her before.

A great many things hadn't occurred to her before. "If I do, I'll fix it myself. You're off duty, Sloan. As of now."

The faintest of smiles graced his thin lips as he retreated from the room. "Very good, Miss."

She didn't quite like the sound of that, either, Court-

ney thought. "Miss" sounded too much like "missing."
She'd been missing a great deal from her life these past
few years. Losing her father was just the beginning of
the wake-up call. Pretending to be part of a family had
brought it all home to her. It had crystallized exactly
what was lacking in her life.

This was what she wanted. To have a family, a husband, a child, people to love who loved her in return,
not because they had to or wanted something, but just
because they wanted to.

Of course, John didn't love her, but it was evident
that Katie did. Enough to get her hooked on the feeling.
Maybe someday, if she was very, very lucky, she would
have the feeling on a permanent basis.

It was something money couldn't buy.

Her father's words rang in her head. This was what
he'd meant, what he'd wanted for her. Love that had no
boundaries, no price tags.

"Too bad I didn't listen to you earlier, Daddy. You
were right." She hoped somehow he could hear her.

The telephone rang, breaking into her thoughts.
Mandy, she thought. When she had postponed her lunch
this morning, Mandy had been too sleepy to think of a
new day to reschedule. Mumbling something under her
breath, she'd promised to get back to her by eight tonight.

Mandy's version of noon, Courtney thought with a
smile. She picked up the receiver, prepared to sink into
the comfort of a nice, long conversation with the only
person she trusted well enough to regard as a confidante.

"Hello?"

She was caught completely off guard by the baritone
voice. "So, tired of him yet, Courtney?"

It took her only a moment fit the voice with a face.

But even as she did, Courtney hoped she was mistaken. "Andrew?"

The deep chuckle erased any doubts. There'd been a time when she had lived for the sound of his voice, the sound of his laughter. But then, there had been a time when she had adored licorice, too. And it turned her stomach now.

"None other."

The best defense, her father had said time and again, was a good offense. Back straightening, Courtney launched hers. "It's been, what, four years? Why are you calling me now?" *Are they fumigating the woodwork where you live?* she thought testily.

"News has it that you're married."

Four years, and the cocky note in his voice hadn't changed one iota. If anything, it had intensified. As if he had anything to be so proud of.

"News is right." She hoped her cold tone was enough to send him scurrying back under whatever rock he had crawled out from under.

"To a gigolo," Andrew concluded. There was pity in his voice, as if he thought the only reason she'd turned to John was to console her aching heart after their breakup. "Really, Courtney, if you were going to throw it all away, I would have thought you'd return to me. After all, I am your kind."

There was that damn word again. "Kind." "He is *not* a gigolo." She struggled to hold on to her temper. She wasn't going to have today spoiled, especially not by some narcissistic cretin who had a money clip where his heart was supposed to be. "And you, Andrew, are not my kind at all."

He didn't believe her. It was there in every word. "Then you've lowered your standards."

"Actually, Andrew," she informed him crisply, "I've raised them since we were together."

"I'd like to test that theory." She could see him in her mind, playacting. How could she have been so stupid as to be taken in by such amateur theatrics? "My life hasn't been the same since you left me, Courtney. There, I've said it. You left me. And wreaked undue havoc on my ego and my heart. But it doesn't have to be over. I'm coming down. Why don't we get together?"

The man was slime. "I'm a married woman now, remember? It's just not possible."

She heard him laugh again. "You don't mean you're going to take your vows seriously, now, do you, Courtney? You never took anything seriously. I should have never let you slip through my fingers."

She knew he sincerely meant that, as if he'd had a prayer of remaining in her life after she'd found out why he was there to begin with—to marry her father's trust fund. His mistake had been in bragging about it to a friend. Hers had been in being blind in the first place.

"You didn't let me slip, Andrew, I ran. As far as I could."

"I've changed, Courtney." Just the right note of pleading entered his voice. He must have been taking lessons from a professional, she thought.

"I've changed, too. I have more common sense now, and I'm a far better judge of character."

She could see him pouting as he huffed. "Well, when you're tired of slumming, you know where to find me."

It was her turn to laugh. "Yes, under the nearest rock." Humor left her mouth. "And now I really have to go."

"Hubby calling?" The question was patronizing.

She decided to rub it in. For old times' sake. "As a matter of fact, he is."

With that, she hung up. Courtney blew out a breath, trying to come to terms with her anger. Calming down wasn't easy when she desperately wanted to wring Andrew's neck. The nerve, the unmitigated nerve of that man, thinking that just because he'd shed crocodile tears, she would be eager to forget her vows and come running.

Never mind that the vows were only words. Andrew didn't know her marriage was in name only.

She thanked God she'd been spared the misfortune of marrying him. Though she hadn't thought so at the time, things did have a way of working out for the best. Maybe there was a guardian angel watching out for her, after all. And if there was, she thought, she could just picture him. With silver-white hair, a cherubic expression and a cigar clenched in his teeth.

"Who was that?"

Courtney swung around, startled. John was standing in the doorway with the oddest expression playing across his face. He looked as if he were angry. Angry and something more. Now what?

"Andrew," she answered.

She didn't expect the name to mean anything to him and she really didn't want to elaborate. All she wanted to do was forget the man had ever surfaced.

She looked guilty, John thought. He felt something sharp twist in his gut. "An old...friend?"

She pressed her lips together as she glanced at the telephone. "I wouldn't exactly call him that."

It wasn't any of his business who called her, or why. He knew where he was going with this, but he couldn't stop himself. "Then what would you call him, exactly? Maybe lover is a more appropriate word?"

Her eyes narrowed as John's tone finally registered. "And if he was, what business is that of yours?"

He had his answer. Rage flared suddenly with the speed of an exploding gas tank, surprising the hell out of him. It was all he could do to maintain a calm exterior. After all, she'd been perfectly clear in the beginning exactly where the lines were drawn and what they were.

And where he stood in relation to them. He'd even wanted it that way. Then.

"None." His tone was flat, dead. "The contract between us is perfectly clear. You get to run off and sleep with whomever you want whenever the whim hits you."

The taste in his mouth was foul. Almost as foul as the emotions running through him. He was jealous. It was easy enough to recognize the sensation. But he shouldn't be, John insisted silently. She wasn't his to be jealous of.

It didn't help. The words were coming of their own volition. All he could do was stand there and listen to himself, the same as she.

"I just didn't think you'd do it so soon, that's all. But then, I never could figure your kind out."

Confusion gave way to hurt and found its home in anger. He saw it all wash over her face, one after the other, like previews of a movie.

What kind of madness had ever possessed her to have feelings of any kind for him? "I am sick to death of hearing that term. Your kind. Your kind," she shouted at him. "For your information, Andrew tells me *you're* not my 'kind.' Well, I've got a news flash for both of you, I don't have a 'kind.'"

He wanted to shake her for making him feel this way.

At the very least, he wanted to walk out and never come back. But he couldn't.

For more than just the reasons that had brought him into this unholy merger to begin with.

He damned her for hurting him. For having the power to hurt him. He felt as if the very air had been snatched away from him. "How about Andrew, isn't he 'your kind'?"

They were alike, he and Andrew, she thought, struggling to hold on to whatever composure she had left. Except that, somehow, hearing what Gabriel had to say hurt even more than anything she'd endured because of Andrew. She didn't know why.

"He thinks so. He wanted to get together this weekend."

He was right, John thought. He had walked in on her making plans for an assignation. And it sliced through him like a rapier, drawing blood instantly. "So, when are you going?"

She didn't owe him an explanation. She didn't owe him a damn thing except for a check.

"I'm not," she retorted. Although maybe she should, she thought now. Maybe...no, that was crazy. She wasn't about to do something self-destructive just because John had turned out to be a louse.

"Got something better lined up?" He hated himself for asking. Moreover, he didn't even recognize himself. Even at the height of the arguments with Diane, he had never felt this torrent of emotion assaulting him, had never experienced this degree of betrayal.

"Yes, I do," she snapped back. "I promised Katie I'd take her to the zoo."

He hadn't expected to hear his daughter's name in

this. John could only stare at Courtney and repeated dumbly, "The zoo?"

"Yes, the zoo, where they keep the four-legged animals." She sucked air into her lungs. "We decided that while you were in line buying lunch this afternoon." Courtney remembered the little girl's gleeful reply when she'd asked Katie if she wanted to go to the San Diego Zoo. "We were going to ask you to come along if you were good. You blew it, mister." She drew herself up, her eyes growing into blue flames. "Now if you'll excuse me, I'm going to bed."

With that, Courtney stormed from the room without a backward glance.

Seething, she ran up the stairs to her room. It would have done her a world of good to slam the door in her wake, but she couldn't. The noise would wake Katie up.

Courtney covered her face with her hands. Her life had been turned completely upside down in less than a month. Now she couldn't even have a decent tantrum in her own house without worrying about the repercussions.

She felt angry tears forming. Furious, she brushed them away. More came to take their place.

The bastard, who the hell did he think he was, taking that attitude with her? He had no right to sit in judgment of her. No right to make her feel this angry.

This miserable.

She couldn't catch her breath. But she did catch a glimpse of her own reflection. A reflection that told her a great deal. More than she wanted to know.

She knew that face. Worse than that, she knew what it meant.

Oh, God, it wasn't happening again. It couldn't be. She couldn't have feelings for him. Not real feelings. Tears were rising in her throat, making her breath hitch.

No!

She refused, absolutely refused, to feel anything for John Gabriel except contempt. He was a boor, an insufferable, manipulative, mercenary boor. How could she feel anything for him? She knew why he was here. For the money. He was doing it only for the money.

She was buying herself a two-year headache, that's what she was doing.

No, she amended, now it was just one year, three hundred and—

Her head jerked up when she heard the knock on her door. Courtney froze, staring at it. Maybe Sloan had decided not to go out after all and had been drawn by the sound of raised voices. It couldn't be Gabriel. He wouldn't dare.

"Who is it?"

"John." The anger had been completely siphoned from his voice, replaced by something she couldn't recognize. Not that she cared. "Can I come in?

There was no way she was letting him in. One look at her face and he'd think she was crying over him instead of over the fact that justifiable homicide couldn't be stretched to cover these circumstances.

Sniffling, she wiped the tear tracks from her cheeks with the back of her hand. It was a stupid trait, to cry when she was angry. Absolutely stupid.

"No," she shouted. "Stay out."

The door opened, anyway. John crossed the threshold and closed the door behind him quietly.

She stared at him incredulously. "What part of 'no' don't you understand?"

In reply, he raised his hands to fend off her words, and anything else she might have wanted to throw his way. "I just wanted to come in to apologize."

She crossed her arms before her. If he thought he could erase what had happened with a single word, he was more deluded than she'd thought. "Fine. You've done it. Now go."

John didn't move. "I can't. That's just the trouble."

Courtney was in no mood for this. She didn't want to see him, not in her room, not in her life. When she thought of what a fool she had been turning into because of him, she could just scream.

"Then I'll just have to shove you out, won't I?" Before he could answer, she was behind him, her hands on his back, as if she really would push him out of her room. But then her hands slid down to her sides. "Damn you, anyway!"

He heard the tears in her voice. John turned and took her hands in his. He had to explain it to her, and maybe, in so doing, he could explain it to himself, as well.

"Courtney, when I heard you on the phone with him—"

"You were eavesdropping—?" He had just added spying to the list of charges against him. How could he?

John shook his head. "I came down to thank you for making Katie so happy today."

He had always thought that he was enough for Katie, that he could be all things to her. But seeing her with Courtney showed him that he'd been wrong. Katie needed a woman's influence in her life. And as she grew, so would that need.

"By the time I realized you were on the phone, I was already listening to what you were saying." It cost him to admit this, but the apology wouldn't be complete if he didn't. "Listening, and getting angry."

She opened her mouth to retort, but he wouldn't let

her. If she interrupted, he'd never find the courage again to finish.

"Before you say anything, I know I don't have any right to get angry, but emotions aren't easily reined in by common sense." The limb he had gone out on was incredibly thin and bending now under the added weight of his admission. But she had a right to know. "If they were, I wouldn't be feeling what I am."

"Angry," she supplied. Any fool could see that.

"Yes," he said tentatively.

That wasn't all, she realized. The breath stopped in her throat. "And?"

Angry words he could say easily. But baring his soul was another matter. He lightly glided his palms along her bare arms. Even touching her like this stirred him.

"I want you, Courtney. I don't want to want you, but I do."

He was pulling her toward him and trying to push her away at the same time. She laughed softly and shook her head. "Well, no one can ever accuse you of having a silver tongue."

"I'm not trying to seduce you..." That wasn't entirely true and he'd promised himself to be honest. "Well, yeah, maybe I am. But what I'm really trying to do is explain to you why I acted like a jerk down there." He had to hurry, before his courage flagged.

"Because suddenly I had a mental image of you going to someone else. Leaning into someone else the way you leaned into me when I kissed you." He looked into her eyes, knowing he was admitting far too much. "I didn't want you doing that. Didn't want you kissing someone else. Didn't want you making love with someone else when you can't make love with me."

She would have been able to walk away from anything else but this. She searched his eyes and saw herself mirrored in them. Trapped there. "I can't?"

Slowly, he shook his head. "No, you can't. Shouldn't." Inch by inch, he felt himself weakening, giving in. Surrendering. As if his hands belonged to someone else, he watched them slip around her waist. "Just like I shouldn't be holding you this way." Unable to help himself, he buried his face in her hair, inhaling deeply. "Or smelling your hair."

Struggling for some measure of control, John moved Courtney away from him to look into her eyes. "Or wanting you so much that I can't even breathe."

The smile on her lips began in her eyes. "Then how did you manage to smell my hair?"

The invitation was there, in her eyes. And he accepted, knowing this was a part of the bargain he should have never agreed to. He laughed, drawing her to him again. "Perverse to the end."

"Not the end." On automatic pilot now, Courtney rose on her toes and wound her arms around the back of his neck. "Not yet." If she was lucky, the end was on the other side of tomorrow.

An eternity from now.

It was all the lead-in he needed.

He brought her to him, his mouth to hers. And with it, his soul.

Everything he couldn't say aloud to her was there, in his kiss, in the way he held her. In the way he looked at her. The very touch of his mouth made love to her a thousand ways, ways she'd never experienced before or even dreamed of.

He made her feel like something precious, something desired. She could feel the passion that was there, locked away, just a step out of reach. And she knew that he was holding himself in check to give her what she needed. Tenderness.

Something within Courtney sobbed with joy.

Pressing herself to him more closely, she slanted her mouth against his, her desires multiplying at a prodigious rate.

He seemed to know what she was thinking even before she did. Knew just how to hold her to reduce her to a state that was somewhere between solid and vapor. It wasn't something well rehearsed and polished, it was something that came from the heart.

She felt like heaven to him. Pure heaven. His hands worshipped her as they slid along the curves of her body, the enticing swell of her breasts. He schooled himself to take her slowly, inch by inch, even as his mind urged him to race, to take her before he woke up from this dream.

But if it was a dream, somehow he would find a way to make it last a little while longer.

They had the night and it stretched out before them, endless, with only their fire to give light to the darkness that lay beyond.

John framed Courtney's face, kissing her over and over again, a starving man at a feast, savoring every individual morsel he discovered. He filled his hands with her hair, snapping the band that had held it in place. Streams of gold rained along his fingers.

Cupping the back of her head, he deepened the kiss and tasted the moan that came from deep in her throat.

Excitement roared in his ears. In his veins. In his loins.

His heart raced wildly in his chest as he felt her eager fingers fumbling at the buttons on his shirt. She was undressing him, her eyes on his. There was so much emotion there, it overwhelmed him.

Courtney dragged the shirt from his shoulders, wanting to press herself against him, but he held her back. As she looked at him in confusion, he undid the tie at the back of her neck. She shivered as the hot-pink halter split in half, each side slipping down her chest until there was only a bit of cloth lingering on the swell of her breasts.

She held her breath as she watched him. John moved the material slowly aside, wonder in his eyes. A child at Christmas, unwrapping the one gift he had wanted with all his might, the one gift he'd been so certain wouldn't be his.

The halter pooled at her waist a moment before he tugged it from her. His eyes skimmed over her. She felt warm each place his eyes touched.

"You are perfect."

"No," she said, bringing her mouth back to his, "I'm not." Because perfect people didn't make mistakes, and she was making one. Somewhere in the recesses of her mind, she knew that. But for now, she didn't care. For now, all she wanted was to feel him, to have him.

She pressed her breasts against his smooth skin, glorying in the heat she felt generated there.

Courtney moaned again, shivering in anticipation as she felt him easing the button on her shorts out of its hole. The zipper parted, a fraction of an inch at a time, fueling the fire in both their veins.

And then she was standing there before him, wearing the most enticing piece of white lace he'd ever seen. White lace trimming tiny red underwear.

His grin was slightly lopsided, and endearing for just that reason. "You look like a Valentine."

Make love with me, now. Before I burst. "A little late in the season for that."

He shook his head. "Never too late for Valentine's Day."

As he took her into his arms again, he could feel her struggling to undo his jeans. He was about to help her, then stopped. Feeling her fingers skimming along his abdomen caused such inexplicably delicious sensations to go through him. His stomach muscles quivered, but he couldn't move. All he could do was feel.

In unison, their hands spreading on one another, they shed the last cloth barriers between them, movement for movement, as if they were holding their breath, anticipating the explosion that was just beyond.

Chapter Twelve

It was, Courtney supposed when she thought of it later, as close to an out-of-body experience as she would ever have. Because part of her was sure that she had died and gone to heaven.

Cradled in his arms, irrevocably lost in his kiss, she felt John lay her back on the bed. Beneath her, the soft, silken covers whispered along her skin. And against her body was the press of his, hard and urgent. Stirring her, making her want him with an intensity that was stunning.

The lovemaking was so slow, so languid, and yet so intense, that she felt she was both inside and outside the circle of participation at the same time. Courtney could see what was coming next, intuit it, but even knowing didn't prepare her for the actual sensation, nor the impact that it had on her.

The impact *he* had on her.

She was drowning in him, in the tenderness that was there in every movement. In the desire she felt throbbing just below the surface.

It aroused a level of passion within her that she had no idea she was capable of. He made her wild, with needs that cried out to be fulfilled.

Aroused to almost a frenzy, she ran her hands along his body in response, in initiation. Courtney didn't want to be the only one overwhelmed with these feelings. She wanted him to share them with her. They were too glorious to be kept to herself.

No matter what she did, John outdid her. And undid her.

How could she have ever thought of him as a rough, rude clod? His movements, so graceful, so lyrical, belonged to a prince, not a commoner. She was the commoner here, an awestruck peasant with her nose pressed against the window of a place she hadn't even dreamed existed. She wanted to be part of it more than she had ever wanted anything else in her life.

John caressed her with his eyes, with his hands, with his lips. Her body burned as he anointed her. Parted where he touched her. Twisted in greedy hope of garnering more.

She felt radiant, beautiful, and was filled with such insatiable desire it took her breath away.

Courtney took his breath away. The attraction he had felt from the first moment he'd seen her exploded in his veins, hot and demanding the instant they came together in her room. It was everything he could do to keep himself in check, to give her what he felt she deserved.

What was to be could not be hurried, no matter what the urgency drumming through his body demanded.

He touched, he explored, he possessed. And in possessing, became completely possessed. Completely hers.

Whatever controls he prided himself on were stripped from him, not layer by layer, but in one huge sweep. He was drunk with wanting, and with the rush that anticipation brought.

For this small moment in time, he would have her. And she would have him. It was more than enough.

And then, when his body begged for release, when his ability to hang on was completely gone, he came to her. Hands linked to hers, he lowered himself into her slowly, watching her eyes as they became one. Truly one for a tiny portion of time.

He watched her eyes and found his soul trapped there.

The rhythm that they moved to, first slowly and then more urgently, was theirs alone and bound them to each other forever as they took the last summit together.

Eventually, pulses slowed and breaths were caught and evened out. The euphoria receded, like an evening shadow merging into the darkness.

Rolling off, John gathered Courtney to him and was surprised at how comforting it felt to have her like this, against him, her heart beating in time with his.

But Surprise had a twin and its name was Worry. John suddenly feared that he could become accustomed to this feeling, to this situation. That perhaps, even now, he was already on that path. And he knew where that path would ultimately lead.

To disappointment. Disappointment so sharp, his very existence would be threatened.

This isolated incident, wonderful though it was, was only an aberration, he told himself. Just an anomaly born of such intense desire that it couldn't be resisted. But once the passion cooled, they would go on being who they were, people born on opposite sides of a phantom class structure that would eventually tear them apart.

It had happened that way before. Why should anything have changed just because he was older?

He didn't want to think about it, not now. Not while she still lay beside him, warm with his love. Sighing, he tucked a loose strand of hair behind her ear.

Courtney looked spent, he thought. As was he. But, heaven help him, he wanted her again. Wanted to see her eyes darkening with desire, wanted to feel her lips racing along his skin. Wanted to feel her moving against him, a cry caught in her throat.

What had she done to him?

She stirred beside him and murmured something he didn't quite make out. Maybe it was just as well. John smiled at her, sadness outlining his mouth, his heart.

"Sorry."

Courtney turned toward him, her heart quickening. Was he sorry they had made love? Now that it was over, did he regret doing this? Was that what he was saying? She didn't think she could bear it if it was.

"Are you asking, or telling?"

There was something guarded in her eyes, he thought. Though their souls had joined briefly, they were far from together now.

"Asking," he told her. *For now.*

She raised herself up on one elbow, her hair spilling over her shoulders, a single strand lingering enticingly over one breast. John's eyes were drawn there first, and then his hand. He couldn't resist cupping the creamy skin.

Courtney felt her breath hitching in her throat all over again as the heat of his hand spread along her body. It sparked a fresh serving of desire in her very core.

"How could I be sorry? That was the most absolutely incredible experience of my life." The flush in her cheeks was part longing, part embarrassment. Sometimes, she talked too much. "I suppose it's not very sophisticated of me to admit that, but then, I never abided by the rules. If my father were still alive, he could tell you that."

If her father were still alive, John thought, then he wouldn't have been here. There would have been no inheritance to gain and she would have had no need of him.

She wouldn't need him forever. He had to remember that.

Remembering didn't negate what he was feeling now. He could have devoured her and still remained unsated. He hadn't thought it was possible to want someone so much immediately after having her. She'd done something to him, tripped off some circuitry that he couldn't seem to shut off.

Because it was so inviting, he pressed a kiss to her throat. He felt her pulse quiver beneath his lips. The quiver passed right through him. "All right, so now what?"

He was talking about the future. She could only think of the night ahead. A night she didn't want to spend alone.

Striving for nonchalance, she succeeded only marginally. It was hard to think with his hand massaging her like that, clouding her mind, robbing her tongue of words.

"You could spend the night," she finally managed, somewhere between a moan and a whimper. "After all, as my husband, you're supposed to be here. Even Katie thinks you're supposed to be here."

It was because of Katie that he was here, but this was between only the two of them. His hand dropped from her breast as he looked into her eyes.

"And what do *you* think?"

Courtney lay back on the bed again and raised her arms to him. "I think you ask too many questions," she whispered.

Maybe he did at that, John thought, covering her mouth with his own. Maybe he thought too much. And right now, all he ached for was to feel.

The place beside Courtney was empty when she woke up the next morning. The thought penetrated her consciousness even before she opened her eyes. He was gone. The sheet on his side beneath her hand was cool.

Still half-asleep, she was aware of a sense of bereavement, of loss, seeping into her. It threatened to rob her of the last remnants of euphoria that still clung to her. She hung on to them with the tenacity of a shipwreck survivor grasping the last piece of driftwood.

Being with John was life-sustaining.

She hadn't slept very much. *They* hadn't slept very much, she amended, a deep smile of satisfaction spreading over her lips.

Last night, she'd called him an incredible lover. The word incredible wasn't nearly adequate enough.

Just thinking of him, of their night together, made her anxious to greet the rest of the day. To find him and be with her. She felt as if she were a schoolgirl again, she thought, kicking back the covers.

No, she'd never felt like this, she realized. Not even when she'd thought herself in love.

Humming, Courtney hit the floor moving, determined to shower and dress in record time.

Unlike Mandy, who could spend hours at her vanity, debating between two shades of the same eyeshadow, Courtney had always had the ability to get ready quickly. Her hair was just barely dry as she hurried out of her room.

She was still flying high on the residual fumes of just barely extinguished passion when she passed John's room. The sound of his voice brought Courtney to almost a skidding halt in front of his door.

He hadn't gone downstairs yet. It was nearly eight. Maybe she was rubbing off on him, as well.

The thought made her smile.

She debated just walking in, then decided not to get ahead of herself. Just because she had luxuriated in the breath-stealing sight of his hard, unadorned body didn't mean she had a right to invade his privacy. There were still spaces to respect.

Courtney raised her hand to knock. A fragment of the conversation coming through the door brought the light plane she was in crashing down to earth. Her heart stilled in her chest as she listened.

"I can't believe this is really happening, Rick. I can't wait to get my hands on her again. Those classic lines, that sleek body—I just don't have the words to describe it. And when I'm in her, I feel like a million dollars." He laughed. "Give or take a hundred thousand or so."

Something twisted inside of her, making her sick.

He was bragging. John was bragging to his best man about making love with her. Courtney felt like throwing up.

How could he?

He'd turned out to be exactly what she'd thought he was when he had accepted her bargain. Someone out for her money, nothing else. If it took making love with her to earn more, so be it.

For a while, she'd been lulled into not examining things, not seeing them for what they were. Like a fool, she'd begun to believe that he had pride. She'd even made up excuses for him in her mind, thinking that if he took her money, there had to be some reason for it. Some noble reason that had nothing to do with greed and that she could understand, even sympathize with.

Talk about never learning from your mistakes! She had to be at the head of the class. Hell, she could teach the damn class, she thought angrily.

It had been just an act on his part. She was only a means to an end for him. And here he was, bragging about it to Rick.

She could have killed him.

Furious, hurt beyond words, Courtney pounded on the door and nearly fell into the room when it gave way. He'd left his door unlocked.

John turned around, startled by her unceremonious entry. He'd left her sleeping in her bed, looking like an angel. An angel he was falling in love with. The last thing he'd expected was to see her come crashing into his room like an avenging Fury.

"Courtney, what are you—?"

He had no right to ask questions. That was her prerogative. "How dare you?" she cried. "How dare you brag?"

He had absolutely no idea what she was talking about. John covered the receiver's mouthpiece, staring at her as if she'd lost her mind. "What?"

The bastard actually had the nerve to play innocent. It wouldn't wash, not after what she'd just heard.

"How dare you brag about—about—" Courtney's

voice broke under the weight of the tears she refused to give him the satisfaction of seeing.

Grasping at the words she flung at him so accusingly, he still had no idea what had made her so angry. "I'm not bragging."

Furious, Courtney gestured at the receiver in his hand. "Oh, no, then what are you talking about?"

"My car," he answered.

"Your car," she echoed. It was her turn to be confused. She was afraid of being taken down another primrose path, even though she wanted so desperately not to believe what she'd heard.

But she knew what happened when she turned a blind eye to things. And she didn't intend to play the fool ever again, not for anyone.

"My car," he repeated. Though the subject was dear to him, the words followed each other slowly as he tried to make sense of her actions. "Actually, it's Rick's father's car. Rick inherited it from him and now he's decided to sell it to me. I've been tinkering with it since I was in college, so it's almost as if it were part mine, anyway."

It sounded plausible, but that might have been because she wanted to believe him. "And how are you going to pay for this car?"

"Slowly." Rick was in no hurry for the money, thank goodness. Otherwise, he'd have to pass. Every cent from the bargain he had struck with Courtney, every cent he had available right now, was earmarked for Katie and her operation.

John held the phone out to her, his eyes darkening. "You want to verify my story?"

Courtney looked down at the receiver. It was a test. Gabriel was doing this on purpose, she thought, daring her to believe him. To take his word on faith. But she'd taken other things on faith, only to be made a fool of. She just didn't have that much faith left to spare.

She took the receiver from him and placed it to her ear. "Rick?"

The voice on the other end greeted her uncertainly. "Hi, Courtney. Um, what's going on?"

A sinking sensation was beginning to form, but it was too late to back off now. "Nothing much. What are you and Gabriel talking about?"

So, he was Gabriel again, John thought, not John, the way he'd been last night. He noticed that she called him John only when she softened. The woman who called him Gabriel was an adversary, ready to go head-to-head with him over almost everything. The one who called him John was soft and pliant and loving.

The only thing the two had in common was that they were both vulnerable.

"My '65 Caddy," Rick answered Courtney. "I just got Gabe to take it off my hands. It's really more his, anyway. And he loves it. It's just taking up space in my garage."

"I see." Something cold and clammy passed over her. She'd been wrong. "Well, goodbye." Courtney handed the receiver back to John. "Rick said you just bought his car."

"Yes, I know. I did." His face was impassive as he placed the receiver to his ear. "Rick? I'll see you in a little while," he promised, hanging up.

The look in his eyes said it all. She hadn't trusted him and it hurt. A lot. Courtney bit her lip. Part of her just wanted to leave the room. She wasn't good at apologizing.

Now she couldn't find the words. To apologize would make her even more vulnerable than she already felt.

But he had apologized to her last night, she remembered. And it hadn't been easy for him, either. She already knew that words didn't come as glibly to him as they did to other men. Like Andrew and Derrick.

She owed him this. Courtney laced her fingers together and stared at the back of his head. It looked as if every muscle in his body was shutting her out.

Courtney took in a deep breath, then jumped in. "I'd like to apologize."

He didn't bother turning around. Instead, he picked up the clothes he had brought in from her room. The clothes, he thought, a fire flaring briefly within him, that she had taken off him. It was hard to reconcile the woman in his room to the one who had been in his arms last night.

"You don't have to apologize." Folding them neatly, he left his jeans on the chair.

"It's just when I heard you bragging, I thought it was about me, about making love with me. I thought you felt I was your trophy and you were showing it off." She took a breath, flustered. He wasn't turning around, damn him. She was standing here, pouring out her heart to the back of his head. "I know that must sound very conceited to you, but you see, it's just that I've been through this before…" Her voice trailed off.

This time he did turn around. Though he said nothing, at least he was listening.

"Oh, I never caught anyone talking about a classic car and thought they meant me." A sad smile played on her lips. "Nothing that entertaining. I just found out that the man I loved, the one I thought loved me, was making arrangements to spend some time with the girlfriend he hadn't brains enough or willpower enough to get rid of. Get rid of?'' She laughed harshly at her own naiveté. ''He promised her that after he married me, there would be a lot more money to lavish on her to make up for his 'unavoidable absences.''''

Her eyes met John's and he saw the pain that he had inadvertently dredged up for her. ''That's what he thought of the time he spent with me. Unavoidable absences from his girlfriend.''

John drew closer to her, but for now, he refrained from taking her into his arms. He knew she wouldn't stand still for pity, so he gave her none. Only his support. ''He was a jerk.''

A ghost of a smile passed her lips. ''I called him a few stronger things. But I thought he had at least taught me a lesson—until I fell in love with Derrick and it happened all over again.'' She shrugged at her own stupidity. ''Different name, different circumstances, same end result. He was making love to my money, not to me. Derrick was very upset when he discovered that my father's will had a clause in it. You know, the one that brought you into my life.''

She said it so cavalierly, he was hard-pressed to guess what she was feeling.

''He was very helpful, though,'' Courtney remembered. ''He offered to arrange for me to marry a working-class friend of his. Was all for it, actually. I think he had something kinky in mind. It upset Derrick terribly when I refused to go along with it. And he *really* became upset when I suggested that we just forget about my so-called inheritance. You see—'' she looked off, unable to look at John as she made her admission ''—Derrick wasn't nearly as well off as I would be with the inheritance. Without it, I just lost my appeal.''

John would have taken her barefoot and penniless. Actually, he would have preferred it that way. But her story explained a great deal. "So when you heard me on the telephone—"

She shrugged again. It had been a natural mistake. "I jumped to a conclusion." Striving to save face, she smiled ruefully at him. "After all, you were talking about classic lines."

He allowed his eyes to skim over her body and thought of the image of her, nude and bathed in moonlight, forever etched into his mind.

"You do have those." His heart went out to her as he brought her into his arms. "Courtney, what happened between us last night isn't available for show-and-tell. I didn't want to have it happen to begin with," he admitted. "I certainly wasn't going to brag about it."

She stiffened, hurt. "I don't remember forcing myself on you."

Though she tried to pull away, he wouldn't let her. She was going to hear him out. If they were going to survive the next two years together, they were going to be nothing but honest with each other.

"With every movement of that beautiful body of yours, you compel me. You are very difficult to resist, Courtney Tamberlaine, even with a track record like mine hanging over my head."

She softened against him, looking up into his eyes. "You never finished telling me about your track record."

John didn't want to go into the whole story now. Besides, it was getting late. "Some other time. I told Rick that Katie and I would be right over. He's taking half a day off, but he does have to get to work."

She didn't know anything about his best friend, a man

she instinctively knew he shared confidences with. Maybe she could start here. "What does Rick do?"

John released her. "He's a detective. Newport Beach." He crossed to the door, then turned and looked at her. Somehow, he'd just expected her to follow. But he realized now that she wouldn't. Not without an invitation. "Would you like to come along?"

She grinned. "I thought you'd never ask."

He hadn't thought he was going to. Not until he'd turned around. Looking at her face, he couldn't help himself.

He put his hand out to her. "Well then, let's not keep him waiting any longer."

Chapter Thirteen

It looked like a butterfly on valium.

John sighed in exasperation as he undid the two ends of his black bow tie for what seemed like the twentieth time. He had no idea why he had to wear one of these things. Or why he even had to come along to the fund-raiser in the first place. It wasn't as if Courtney really needed him.

He muttered under his breath and tried again.

Katie walked in through the adjoining bathroom, her hand firmly tucked in Courtney's as she pulled the woman in her wake.

"I helped Mommy fix her hair." She pointed proudly to Courtney's upsweep, zeroing in on an area. "I pushed that pin in, there."

John caught the look in Courtney's eyes in the mirror and smiled. "Did she draw blood?" he asked quietly.

"Just about," she whispered. Exercising a sleight of

hand, she'd been able to rearrange the bobby pin Katie had pushed deep into her hair without the little girl noticing.

Katie was scrambling onto the chair next to the bureau. She beckoned her father over, her eyes on the limp tie.

"I can do that, Daddy. I can help you, too."

She probably couldn't do any worse than he was right now, John thought. He stopped fumbling with the bow tie and leaned over toward Katie.

"If you really wanted to help me, you'd get me out of this shindig."

The bow was clearly proving harder to master than she'd thought. Katie frowned, her brows drawn together in deep concentration. "What's a shindig?"

Still bowed over, he slanted a look at Courtney before answering. "It's an old-fashioned word that means letting someone dig your grave for you, starting at shin level."

Katie blew out a breath and began reworking the bow. She looked just like her father when she did that, Courtney thought fondly.

"Very funny. Don't listen to him, Katie. He just likes to complain." Courtney paused, debating whether or not to offer her assistance. She didn't want the little girl feeling she was usurping her place with her father. But they couldn't stay here all night, either. "Need any help with that?"

Katie nodded solemnly. "It's not working," she lamented. She let the ends drop. "I'm not very good at it."

"That's only because you need practice," Courtney assured her. "Here, let's give it another try."

Rather than moving her aside, Courtney stood behind

the little girl and covered the small hands with her own. Very carefully, she guided Katie's movements, threading her own fingers in where she could. It was awkward that way and took twice as long, but a bow finally emerged that could have passed even the strictest judge's approval.

Courtney stepped back, gesturing at their handiwork. "See? Practice."

Pride shone in Katie's smile as she took her father's hand to assist her descent from the chair. She turned toward Courtney. "We did it."

Courtney leaned down and pressed her forehead against Katie's. "*You* did it. I just hung around and helped a little."

She glanced up. John was just standing there, watching the two of them. Watching her. And making her toes curl and her skin heat.

So what else was new?

She nodded toward John as she whispered to Katie, "Doesn't he look good?"

Katie's expression was somber. "Very good."

John waved a hand at the compliment. He could feel the bow tie cutting off the circulation to his neck already. It had nothing to do with the actual tightness of his tie. It was the mere existence of the tie that did it. Even while he'd worked as an engineer, he'd avoided all contact with ties unless it was absolutely necessary.

"Well, 'he' feels miserable." He looked at his reflection. All he saw was a very unhappy-looking guy who was much more at home in jeans and a work shirt. "Why can't you just have a barbecue?"

She laughed, adjusting his collar for him. "Because you don't get people to fork over a thousand dollars a plate for hamburgers, coleslaw and baby-back ribs."

"Plates sure cost a lot," Katie declared with wonder.

"They do when they belong to Courtney," he told his daughter. Fund-raisers had always left him cold. He'd been forced to attend several, all political, while he'd been married to Diane.

"They don't belong to me. They belong to the Children's Foundation for Better Health," Courtney corrected, reciting the name of the hospital her father had founded and underwritten. "Now let's get going."

He glanced at his watch. It was early. The invitations she'd sent out had said the party began at seven. He didn't want to spend any more time mingling with cardboard people than he absolutely had to. "Whatever happened to being fashionably late?"

Courtney smiled. "Someone taught me the value of time." Threading her arm through his, she urged him toward the stairs. Katie gleefully followed. "Besides, I'm in charge of this little 'shindig,' as you called it, and there are probably seven emergencies going on even as we speak."

Courtney stopped at the bottom of the stairs to give him a once-over. "Your tie is tied, your shoes are on. You look gorgeous."

Her point was that he was out of excuses. She wasn't consciously fishing for a compliment, although she would have gladly accepted one. Prior to Katie's arrival into her room, Courtney had dressed very carefully for this function, but not with an eye out to impress any of her guests. All she wanted was for John to notice her. More than that, she wanted to knock his shoes off and burn up his socks.

She had thought that wearing a skintight, hot-pink dress slit dangerously high on her thigh with no back to speak of might just do the trick. But so far, his socks appeared unscorched.

John watched the way the light from the chandelier seemed to bounce off the hot-pink sequins of her gown, adding color to her skin. When she turned to pick up her wrap, he felt his palms itch. The dress was backless and almost sideless, rendering him almost speechless.

He wanted to take her to bed, not to a party. Taking the wrap from her hands, he dropped it around her bare shoulders. "You look pretty gorgeous yourself," he whispered.

His breath slid along her cheek. If she wasn't chairing the function, she would have been sorely tempted to forget about attending. She was, anyway. But duty was something that was ingrained and she couldn't turn her back on it just because he was making her want things. Badly.

She smiled up into his eyes. "I thought you'd never notice."

"Oh, I noticed all right," he assured her. "I always do."

And it was true. He noticed everything about her. He had even before he'd made love with her. But now, it was as if all his senses had been heightened. Usually, you had to lose one sense for the others to become sensitive. But he seemed to have gained one—an infinite sense of her. His other senses had just hurried to keep up.

"Can I stay up and wait for you?" When they turned in unison to look at her, Katie was shifting back and forth on her toes, looking from one to the other, hope dancing in her eyes.

Up to now Courtney had been indulgent with Katie, but she was beginning to understand that loving sometimes meant saying no. She bit her lip, looking at John for guidance. She felt her way through this. "We're going to be back awfully late."

John certainly hoped not. Even staying there an hour was going to be sixty minutes too long.

"Not that late," he countered. He took Katie's chin in his hand, striking a bargain. "Okay, if you promise to take a nap first."

He could feel the pout in his palm as it grew. "Do I have to? I'm a big girl."

She was becoming stubborn, he thought, and wondered if being around Courtney had anything to do with it. In any case, this was nonnegotiable. "If you want to get bigger, you'll nap. Deal?"

She sighed. When Daddy looked like that, there was no way around him. Katie nodded. "Deal."

They left her with Sloan, though John would have rather remained with Katie himself.

"Don't worry, Sloan'll take care of her," Courtney promised as she got into the limousine. "Everyone at the house loves her. It's no hardship taking care of Katie."

He thought of the mind-numbingly dull evening ahead. "Yeah, but who'll take care of me?"

"I will," Courtney said without missing a beat.

"You're going to be busy," he reminded her.

There was no denying that, but it didn't mean they had to be separated. "And you're going to be at my side the entire evening."

She meant it, he thought. Right now, he wasn't certain if that was a good thing. "You really know how to threaten a guy, don't you?"

She laughed, curling up against him in the back seat

as the chauffeur started the car. "You ain't seen nothing yet. Wait until I bring out the rubber hoses."

Because it came so naturally to him, John slipped his arm around her shoulders. "I can hardly wait."

John had never given much thought to the way money was collected to fund the facilities so vital to Katie's well-being. He'd been too concerned with Katie's health to wonder where and how the money was found to build the various wings of a hospital.

It took, he realized now, the combined generosity of the very people he had looked down on all these years with nothing short of contempt. His experience with his ex-in-laws and their friends had colored his perspective of the whole class. Or rather, discolored it.

Now, as he looked from the dais at the sea of well-dressed people sitting at their tables, listening to Courtney deliver an impassioned speech, he was forced to reassess his feelings.

They might be richer than he was, but they were people just the same. People who were moved by the suffering of children they would never know. Moved to donate their time via fund-raisers, and to donate their money.

He hadn't been fair. Not to them, certainly not to Courtney. But a man could learn from his mistakes and make amends. As long as there was breath left in a body, amends could always be made.

He looked back at Courtney as she finished her speech. He had to admit that she'd surprised him. But then, she'd been doing that right from the beginning.

Courtney shifted her note cards, covering them with her hand. She was departing from what she'd prepared. Instead, she looked into her heart. A heart that had opened even wider since Katie had entered her life. Now she could imagine more fully the anguish parents felt, knowing their child was ill with something that wouldn't go away within a day or a week. Ill with something that might shorten their lives and rob them of the joy of growing up.

She thought of how she would feel if something threatened that happy little girl who was waiting up for her at home. Her heart quickened, inspiring her words.

Courtney smiled at the tables, which were filled with people she recognized. People she'd cajoled and coerced into coming to these fund-raisers year after year. Good people.

"Now, I know that you are probably about to consume the most expensive filet mignon you've ever purchased, barring Louis, of course," she paused, gesturing toward the man, "who likes to fly to France for lunch." Her eyes met Mandy's as she laughed. "But, at the risk of sounding a little like a broken record—for those of you who remember vinyl—after dinner I'd like you to open up your checkbooks again as well as your hearts and write yet another check for the foundation."

The smile faded, her eyes growing serious. "We would really like to complete work on that new surgical wing by the end of the year. For some of these children, you are all they have. You are their key to hope in a world that has suddenly been rendered hopeless for them. And some of those children who desperately need the services of the wing under construction won't be able to wait around until I've finished begging and pleading for the money.

"They need the wing yesterday. I'd like to at least promise them that it'll be there in the not-too-distant tomorrow."

And then the smile returned, flitting over as many people as she could make eye contact with. "Now, eat up and then pay up. *Bon appétit.*"

Retreating, Courtney left the podium amid hearty applause. She saw a strange, meditative look on John's face as she stepped off the dais.

This was the first time he'd heard her speak, she thought. She wondered if he'd heard something he found disagreeable. "What?"

She'd moved him. Really moved him. He felt like a heel for what he'd thought of her. "I didn't think you cared that much."

It wasn't a criticism, but an admission. Inch by inch, they were coming along pretty well, she thought in satisfaction. Like any newlyweds. Their marriage didn't feel as much of a sham as it had before.

"There're a lot of things about me you don't know." Her hand in his, she made her way to the head table. "I don't spend all my time watching sexy-looking engineers working on my guest house."

"Lucky for me."

All in all, it wasn't nearly as bad an evening as he'd anticipated. He supposed, in part, that was due to his own attitude. He'd lost it. He was no longer looking at Courtney's "kind" as bored, rich people with time and money weighing heavily on their hands, people who contributed nothing useful to society. If not for them, places like Harris Memorial, the hospital where Katie had been treated since she was born, wouldn't have existed. Or, if it had, it would have been woefully underprepared to attend to Katie's special needs.

And then, of course, there was Courtney. She hadn't let him hang back. Rather than leaving him cooling his heels, Courtney incorporated him in every facet of the evening, never leaving his side except for when she delivered her speech. And even then, he had been only a few feet away.

He didn't mind. He liked being near her. Liked, too, having his eyes opened to his mistakes. And he had been mistaken about Courtney. Badly mistaken.

With the pride of a new bride, a role that seemed to be becoming increasingly easier for her to play, Courtney introduced John not only to more of her friends, but also to some of the doctors on the staff at the Children's Better Health Hospital.

John's mind swam with names and faces as he tried to remember each one.

One he didn't have to try.

"And this is Dr. Darel Benjamin," Courtney told him. "Dr. Benjamin has just graciously accepted a position on our hospital staff, as well as continuing to attend his patients at Harris Memorial. Dr. Benjamin, this is my husband, John Gabriel."

The bearded, distinguished physician looked at John in surprise as they shook hands. "Well, I certainly didn't expect to see you at one of these, John."

John didn't risk looking at Courtney, afraid his expression would make him look guilty. He didn't want her finding out this man was Katie's doctor. His daughter's health was still his problem to handle. His and Katie's.

"It's part of my husbandly duties," he said glibly, looking around for a way out.

Benjamin looked at the couple before him thoughtfully. "I'm afraid I'm a little confused. When did you two marry?" He addressed his question to John.

"Recently," John answered before Courtney could

say anything. He wanted to get her away before Benjamin mentioned anything about the upcoming surgery. "If you'll excuse us, Doctor."

Not waiting for a reply, John took Courtney's arm, drawing her to the other side of the room.

She felt as if they were running from something. "What was that all about?"

Courtney glanced back at the doctor, now engaged in conversation with Rita Hennessy. The older woman was undoubtedly pumping him for free advice regarding her imagined heart condition. Rita loved coming to these functions and buttonholing doctors for free advice, which was fine with Courtney. The woman always donated generously when the time came.

She turned her attention to John. "Where do you know Dr. Benjamin from?"

John picked up a glass of wine. He had refrained all evening, but now he felt as if he needed a drink.

"Diane." He deliberately avoided her eyes. "He was—is, I imagine," he corrected himself, "Diane's father's doctor." He'd had no contact with either in-law since the divorce, except for Diane's funeral. That had hardly been the time to exchange pleasantries or play catch-up.

He figured his explanation would satisfy Courtney. The initial referral actually had come from Diane's father. Benjamin had been the specialist called in when fetal distress had turned out to have a name. Ventricular Septal Defect. A large name for a very small hole in the wall of the lower chambers of Katie's heart.

It really was a small world, Courtney thought. She felt bad, subjecting John to the unexpected meeting. "I can see how that would have made you feel awkward."

He had endured the evening without complaint and

had even been entertaining to some of her friends. She saw new respect emerging in their eyes. And something more than tolerance in his. This had shaped up to be one of the more successful evenings of her life.

It was time to take pity on him.

Courtney took his arm. "I'm tired, how about you?"

Now that she mentioned it, he did feel pretty wrung out. "Yeah."

"Then let's go home."

John was surprised by her suggestion. And more surprised at himself when he didn't jump at it. "Aren't you supposed to stay until the end?"

Technically, he was right. She had always been the last one out the door since she had taken the position over from her father. At first it was because she'd had something to prove, and later it was because she truly believed in the cause she was involved in.

But now she had other responsibilities. "Mandy can handle everything," she told him.

He looked across the floor and saw the petite brunette. Surrounded by men he had a feeling she had hand-selected, Mandy was carrying on an animated conversation with all of them.

"Mandy?" The question was enveloped in a laugh.

But Courtney was serious. "She's really very good. She can separate a man from his money faster than a mosquito can draw blood. It's rather humbling to watch."

Courtney's eyes were drawn in the same direction as his. But she saw what he couldn't. It might look like simple flirtation, but Mandy was at work, promoting the hospital.

"I just got the position as chairwoman because my father started the foundation. If it was assigned according to merit, the position probably would have gone to Mandy. I made her my assistant. Let me go tell her we're leaving." A smile played on her lips. "Unless, of course, you want to stay."

He shook his head, already thinking of the night that was still ahead for them. "No, four hours is about my limit."

John followed her, glad to be leaving, but glad he had come, as well. For, by coming, he'd gotten to see Courtney in her element, her true element. Watching her at work had added dimension to her for him. He realized that she had never really been the spoiled heiress he'd imagined her to be. There had been a generous side to her all along.

Knowing that was going to make leaving her all the more difficult when the time came.

But the time wasn't now, he reminded himself. Now, he had more pressing things on his mind. She was coming to his bed tonight. Nothing had been said. He just knew.

"It's getting a little crowded," Courtney said over her shoulder. "You stay here, I'll extricate Mandy from her court."

He watched her disappear into the crowd. Within moments, she'd returned, Mandy in tow.

"All set," she announced. "Mandy's agreed to take my place for me."

Mandy was at his side instantly. Taking his arm, she looked up at John. "Okay, let's go home."

A bemused expression washed over Courtney's face. "Mandy, what are you doing?"

Mandy was all innocence. "Well, you said to take your place. So I am." She wrapped both arms around

John's and fluttered her lashes seductively. "Your place or mine, Johnny?"

Courtney slowly removed Mandy's hands from John's arm as he laughed. "I meant here—take my place *here*."

Mandy snapped her fingers. "Drat. I think you got the better end of the deal," she said wistfully.

"As long as you're swapping partners, mind if I cut in?"

The question came from behind them.

The smile melted from Courtney's lips as she turned around to face Andrew. She didn't remember seeing his name on the list and knew she hadn't invited him. He had to have come as someone's guest.

So much for discerning tastes.

"No one's cutting in anywhere," she informed him coolly.

Andrew began to slip his arm around her shoulders, but Courtney shrugged him off. Anger flashed across his face, then faded into a smirk as he looked at John.

"Aren't you going to introduce us, Courtney?"

"No."

"Ashamed?" he guessed.

She placed her hand on John's chest, anticipating his desire to separate Andrew's head from the rest of him. "No, just tired of you and whatever game you think you're playing."

"No game. I'm just curious to meet the man who finally won your purse strings, that's all."

Firmly moving Courtney aside, John placed himself between her and the man he had taken an instant dislike to. "I'd watch my tone if I were you."

Andrew's eyebrows rose mockingly. "Oh, he's physical, too. But then, I forgot. He works with his hands, doesn't he? Just like Daddy wanted." Andrew circled

John slowly. "I suppose I can see some of the attraction." Standing in front of John, his smirk deepened. "Or what, Mr. Tool Belt? You'll hit me with your level?"

Courtney saw John's eyes darken and knew the look well.

"I won't need a level," he said evenly.

She had to put a stop to this now, before it got out of hand. Courtney placed a restraining hand on each of them, though she wanted to hit Andrew herself. "Andrew, I don't want a scene here."

"Then you shouldn't have come with him." Contempt colored his features. "He's just cramping your usual style."

Mandy took hold of Andrew's arm. "Andrew, they're playing our song. Let's dance." She tried to pull him away.

But he wasn't about to move. "We don't have a song," he snapped. His pride had been stung. Courtney had walked out on him, yet she had married someone like this. "Really, Courtney, when are you going to come to your senses? Whatever he does for you in bed, I can certainly do bet—"

"That does it." Before anyone else could stop him, John swung one well-aimed punch at Andrew's jaw. Andrew crashed to the floor, shouting obscenities. He remained there, holding his face.

John waved his fist to and fro, trying to work through the pain radiating over his knuckles.

The music stopped and everyone looked in their direction.

Mandy quickly stepped over Andrew, waving at the crowd. "And so much for our floor show," she announced. "Now please, go back to what you were doing.

Next show will be in an hour. Jugglers and mimes."
Mandy grinned mischievously. "I promise to cancel
them if you all make another round of donations."

Turning, she looked at Courtney and John, then
shooed them out.

"Go on," she urged. "Make your getaway while you
still can." Mandy winked broadly at John.

Taking her arm, John led Courtney out. He grinned
despite the situation. "I guess you were right about
Mandy. She can handle things pretty well."

Courtney looked down at his hand. The knuckles were
red and skinned. "Hurt?"

His knuckles stung like the devil. "They make it look
really easy in the movies." John glanced over his shoulder as they walked out. "He's the first guy I ever
punched."

"I'll have him bronzed," Courtney promised. "Now
let's just get out of here."

He waited until she had picked up her wrap from the
cloakroom. Helping her on with it, John tried to gauge
her mood. "You're not angry?"

"Angry?" Where would he get that idea? "You just
defended my honor. Why should I be angry?" Actually,
she was secretly thrilled. No one had ever done that for
her before.

John shrugged as they walked outside. "Diane
chewed me out for using the wrong fork at a dinner
party."

She turned to face him. When was he going to understand? "I am not Diane."

He looked into her face, emotions tugging at his heart.
The lines weren't blurred any longer. "No," he agreed.
"You're not."

They found Katie curled up on the sofa when they walked in. Sloan was sitting beside her, an unread magazine laying open on his lap. It looked as if it had been there all evening. Sloan, that old curmudgeon, was completely captivated by the little girl.

He rose to his feet when he saw Courtney come in. The magazine fell to the floor and he stooped to pick it up.

"She's been waiting for you," he whispered.

Courtney crouched down beside the sofa and brushed the hair from Katie's face. She looked like an angel, Courtney thought. "You should have put her to bed, Sloan."

"She refused." And he hadn't had the heart to insist. "Said she wanted to see her 'beautiful Mommy and Daddy' when they returned."

"She really does have a way with words." Courtney laughed.

"Okay, it's off to bed, honey." John gathered Katie in his arms.

Katie stirred, then, still asleep, she placed her arm around his neck. As John began to walk toward the staircase, she sighed. Her eyes fluttered open for a moment.

"Was the party nice?"

Courtney exchanged glances with John. She looked at the bruised knuckles. They contrasted so sharply with the silken head they caressed. Her hero, she thought fondly.

"Yes, it was a very nice party, pumpkin."

"Did you bring me some cake?"

Courtney opened her purse. To John's surprise, she took out a neatly wrapped piece. "Sure did."

"That's good," she murmured, her eyes shutting again.

They both put Katie to bed.

Chapter Fourteen

"Here, let me take a look at that." Courtney reached for John's bruised knuckles as soon as they slipped out of Katie's room.

He didn't want her fussing over him—at least, not over something so inconsequential. Tonight, at the fundraiser, when that jerk in the tuxedo had tried to put moves on Courtney, he had begun to realize just how much he cared for her. How much she had come to mean to him in such an incredibly short time.

John had never been one to lead with his emotions, yet that was just what he had done when Andrew had begun making insulting remarks. He'd allowed his emotions to spill out and get the better of him.

That was when he knew. Courtney had crossed the line between the outside world and the world he had created for himself and Katie. She was in his world now.

He didn't know whether he was happy about that or not.

John drew his hand away. "It's not my best feature."

He could play macho if he wanted, but she wasn't about to be ignored. Courtney took his hand again, this time holding on to it firmly. She looked at it closely. There was a cut, no, two, right across his knuckles. That needed attention.

Still holding his hand, she led him into the connecting bathroom. "No, your best feature would be your sunny personality."

He laughed, sitting down when she silently pointed to the closed commode. He had a hunch that he wouldn't win this round and that resistance would be futile. Just as resisting her had proven to be.

"I wouldn't throw stones if I were you."

Courtney took out the small bottle of peroxide from the medicine cabinet, then searched for cotton balls in the cabinet under the sink. "I guess I really did give you a hard time in the beginning."

He was enjoying the view. The gown adhered to her like a second skin as she wiggled farther into the cabinet. "You could have given lessons to a marine drill sergeant."

Courtney snaked her way out, then sat back on her heels, her prize in her hand. She grinned as she looked at John. "That good, huh?"

He smiled. "No." A few times there, he'd wanted to wring her neck. "But you turned out to be."

She unscrewed the bottle cap. "You're just trying to get my mind off your knuckles."

"Maybe." He didn't think of her as particularly the handy or nurturing type. "Like I said, they're not my best feature. What I am trying to do, in case it's not obvious, is get you into bed.''

Courtney soaked the cotton ball in peroxide. ''If you want to play doctor, let me play nurse first.''

He shrugged, bracing himself. ''Whatever turns you on.'' With an exaggerated leer, he moved his eyebrows up and down. ''I can be the lonely, wounded pilot, shot down over World War II France during a reconnaissance mission.'' Casually, he stroked her thigh with his other hand.

That went right to the heart of it, all right, she thought. Warmth spread out tributaries in all directions. She was done for. ''Feeling your oats, are you?''

There was nothing innocent about the look he gave her. ''I'd rather feel yours.''

She'd never seen him this playful before. The longer she knew him, the more she found to like. ''Boy, hitting Andrew certainly did give you a rush.''

He hadn't thought of it that way, but maybe she was right. ''I guess.'' John shrugged. ''It just felt good shutting his mouth. Like I said, I've never hit anyone before.''

Holding his hand, she slowly dabbed the cotton ball over the cuts. He winced, but said nothing. She hadn't expected him to. He'd probably borne up to his first inoculation the same way, tight-lipped and macho.

''Never been in a fight before?'' Her eyes swept over him. Even the tuxedo couldn't hide the body beneath. ''Just one look at those manly muscles always sent everyone running, huh?''

His knuckles were really stinging. He hadn't realized he'd cut his hand when he hit Andrew. Must have been on his pointy chin, John thought. ''I didn't always have muscles.''

Tossing the cotton away, she raised his hand to her lips and blew softly along his knuckles, drying them. And warming him.

"Tell me about it," she urged.

The thing he liked least in life was talking about himself. He was even less inclined now, when she was unwittingly tying him in knots.

Or was she doing that consciously?

"I just did."

He was being too literal. And too stubborn, she thought. "No, I mean tell me about childhood. Specifically, yours," she elaborated when he said nothing.

John shifted, growing more uncomfortable. What was the point of talking about growing up with an aunt and uncle instead of a mother and father because neither one of them had wanted him? His aunt and uncle hadn't wanted him, either, but they were big on responsibilities. They never missed an opportunity to tell him that, either. He'd lost count how many times they'd reminded him in fifteen years.

He had struck out on his own as soon as he could, using scholarships, student loans and a part-time job as a carpenter to get him to that degree he wanted.

And then he had met Diane and his life had changed forever.

Old news.

"Nothing much to tell." John shrugged, as if he were dismissing a movie that had been too boring to sit through. "I was born, I grew up and here I am."

Courtney screwed the cap back on the peroxide bottle. "Wow, even those outlines that college students use to cheat on their term papers with give you more than that."

She replaced the bottle and tossed the box of cotton

back underneath the sink, her eyes on his, waiting for more.

He didn't want her pity, and he knew he'd arouse it if he told her what she wanted to know. "Maybe they have more to work with."

Planting herself in front of him, she looked down into his eyes, searching for the answers he wouldn't give her. "I really doubt that."

The bathroom light played off her sequins, sending the lights it reflected dancing along his skin. He found himself wanting her all over again, just the way he had more than a dozen times tonight. "You want to spend all night talking?"

"Some of it," she said honestly. There was so much she wanted to know about him. She wanted to hear every scrap of detail he could remember, no matter how minor. "I want to know who I'm kissing."

Instead of answering, he fished his wallet out of the inside of his jacket. Opening it to his driver's license, he handed it to her.

She pushed the wallet back at him, shaking her head. "I had no idea you had such a droll sense of humor." And then she grew serious. "Who are you when you're not being Katie's father and defending my honor?" When he still didn't answer, she tried to get the ball rolling with a basic question. "Why was an engineer rebuilding my guest house?"

Knowing she wasn't going to be put off completely, he gave her the most general of answers and hoped it would temporarily satisfy her.

"I was laid off." Technically, it was true. He had to take so many days off to take care of Katie, he'd lost his job. But those were details he didn't want to share.

"And work in the field is scarce these days, so I had a career change. I like working with my hands.

"Speaking of which, they feel rather empty right now." He placed them on the swell of her hips and drew her to him. "There, that's better."

There was nothing to do but give up. John was clearly not in the mood to open his past to her. But he would someday, she promised herself.

If worse came to worst, she could always get her hands on the report Parsons spoke of. It might be awkward, but she could make up some excuse.

For now, all she wanted was to be taken back to the place they had found within each other. The place where he made her feel so loved, so wanted.

She threaded her arms around the back of his neck, her body leaning temptingly toward him. "I've got something in mind that's even better."

John rose, his body sliding seductively against hers as he gained his feet. They both felt the electricity crackling between them. Calling to them.

"Nice to know we think alike on some things." He'd had enough of talking. Going with his feelings, John covered her mouth with his own.

They had all night.

They wanted this instant.

Passions ignited in a heartbeat, sending them racing to recapture ground they had already consecrated. Somehow, it felt like a race against time.

Maybe, in a way, it was. A race against things that existed just outside them that could ruin everything for them. An inevitability that would ultimately rob them of this paradise they had discovered.

For there were secrets between them.

Courtney had never felt such intense urgency racing

through her as she slid her palms along his chest. She dragged his jacket from his arms, tossing it aside. Her fingers were barely functioning as she fumbled to unbutton his shirt.

As she worked to free his body, he worked to free hers. There was less for him to do. And more frustration.

"Where's the zipper to this damn thing?" John rasped impatiently against her mouth when his search along her back had yielded nothing.

Giddy, Courtney laughed and raised her left arm. "Hidden under here."

It was one of those zippers that was visible only if you knew where to look. It figured. Grasping the end, he tugged on it.

"This was designed by a woman, wasn't it? Made to frustrate a man and make him beg."

And if that's what it took, tonight he was up to it. He could beg if it meant one more night of ecstasy with her.

He'd certainly come a long way, he thought. Or fallen a long way.

The zipper rested on its base. The shining material parted from her body, genuflecting as it went down to the floor.

Courtney shivered in anticipation as she felt the zipper sliding down along her side.

Her laugh was deep, throaty in response to his question. And completely captivating. "How did you know?"

"Just a hunch." The dress fell away, coming to rest around her high-heeled, sandaled feet like a bright pink wave. He could have swallowed his tongue and very nearly did. "You look like a fantasy."

She felt like one. A bright, beautiful, enticing fantasy. Because he made her feel that way.

She could have given him anything. Everything.

Courtney felt the air backing up in her lungs as his hands worshipped her skin, sliding along its curves roughly, bringing her closer to waves of ecstasy even as he managed to hold her back.

She'd all but ripped the clothes off his body to be closer to him, to seal the union that was so vital to her. She didn't remember doing any of it, only the feeling that was driving her.

And when she'd divested him of everything, he was more stunning to her than Michelangelo's David had been to its creator. His mouth took hers, heat searching for heat.

She let herself be enfolded in his hunger, in his passion, ready to be taken quickly. Her body demanded it. Begged for it.

But he surprised her.

Again.

John held off, choosing now to introduce her to the wonders of her own body. He became her teacher and he seemed to know her body far better than she did. He knew its secrets and its releases. And he showed them to her, one by one.

On the bed, as John stroked her, as he kissed her over and over again, he brought her to the brink of one crest, and then another. Each release was more sumptuous than the one before. With the promise of another shimmering just beyond.

She thought she was going to explode.

And when she did, when she thought it couldn't get any better, any richer, it began all over again.

She felt his hands, his hot breath, everywhere along her body as he explored, charted, claimed.

This wasn't fair, her mind cried. She wanted to make

him as crazy as he was making her. Wanted to make him yearn the way she yearned, to toss him in the midst of a fever pitch the way he did her.

But for that she needed strength and he kept sapping hers away from her. For that she needed to tear herself away from his plundering mouth and blaze her own trail along his body. And she didn't want to tear herself away, not yet. Not just yet. Because he was reducing her to a state that was so delicious, so addictive, she couldn't find enough willpower to make herself leave.

A little while longer, everything within her pleaded. She urgently pressed his head against her as she felt the heat of his mouth burning its way along her thighs.

Just a little while longer.

His lips and tongue stole the very life from her. And created it anew. Courtney twisted against his mouth, craving more, needing more, knowing if she had more, she would die.

His hot mouth claimed her one final time as she arched against him, then fell back, too delirious to even know where she was.

When she opened her eyes, it was to see him above her. Courtney felt a smile rising to her lips. It was almost all she had strength for.

"You should punch Andrew more often."

"I will," he promised her, "if he ever lays another hand on you."

How possessive. How territorial.

"My hero," she whispered.

Courtney knew that she should bristle and protest, but something inside of her loved it. And understood. Because she would have done the same to any woman who tried to claim him.

And then he was entering her, filling her not just with

a promise, but with himself. Courtney arched her hips, taking him in deeper, deeper, until he'd reached her very soul.

One by one, he'd joined his hands, his lips, his body, with hers. And she knew, even as her senses rose to a fever pitch, that she wanted it to be this way always. At any cost.

The phone rang, breaking apart a delicious dream she was having, tearing it into fragments that quickly disappeared. She remembered only the passion that it embodied.

Or had that been real?

Courtney opened her eyes, reaching for the telephone mechanically. It was morning. The morning after the annual fund-raiser. The morning after a torrid night of lovemaking.

Only slowly did another, more important fact penetrate. It was morning and the place beside her wasn't empty.

Courtney realized that even as she brought the receiver to her ear.

Her mouth curved as sunshine filled her, coming from a more ethereal source than the one outside her window. John was still here, in her bed, asleep beside her. He hadn't left her this time, but had remained to greet the day with her.

Courtney let out a long, contented sigh.

Progress.

"Hello?" she said sleepily into the receiver. She felt as if she could hug the whole world.

The voice on the other end belonged to a soft-spoken woman. "Is this Mrs. Gabriel?"

Mrs. Gabriel. Courtney rolled the name over in her

mind slowly, savoring it. Until this moment, she hadn't thought of herself as that.

It did have a nice ring to it, didn't it? What if...?

But she was letting her mind drift in directions that weren't completely mapped out yet. There was a danger in getting ahead of herself. Courtney focused her mind back to the present.

"Yes, it is." She dragged her hand through her hair, trying, at the same time, to clear her brain.

"This is the surgical department at Harris Memorial Hospital calling. We're just confirming your daughter's surgery date."

The crisp statement shook the last remnants of sleep and daydream from her. Courtney tried to make sense out of the words. "Her what?"

"Her surgery date," the woman repeated patiently. If she noticed any surprise on the other end, she gave no indication as she competently recited the particulars of Katie's surgery, beginning with the day and time. "We wanted to inform you that her anesthesiologist will be Dr. Cunningham. Her surgeon, of course, will be Dr. Benjamin, and Dr. Swan will be assisting, as usual. They work in tandem, you know," she confided. "And your daughter couldn't be in better hands. There'll be another team on standby. Everything will be ready when she comes in.

"Since you have no insurance, there will be a few extra forms to sign, so please be sure to stop by the preadmit desk first."

"Yes, of course," Courtney heard herself saying hollowly. "Thank you."

The woman said goodbye. Reaching over, Courtney hung up the receiver and then sat there perfectly still, too numbed, too shocked, to move.

John turned around in bed and looked at her. The telephone had woken him, but he had assumed that the call was for Courtney. No one called him here except Rick, and Rick was on duty this morning.

He saw the expression on her face and sat up. "Bad news?"

Only her eyes shifted in his direction. The rest of her was immobilized with disbelief.

Katie was having an operation and he hadn't thought enough of her to tell her. Hadn't thought enough of her to let her come even this far into his life.

Someone had cut off the air supply in her world. Everything ached. The hurt Courtney felt was entirely without precedent and almost more than she could bear.

Something was wrong, he thought. Her face was a frozen mask. He couldn't think of a single thing that could affect her this way. What had happened?

Concerned, John slipped his arm around her shoulders. She was shaking. "Courtney, what is it?"

She was so hurt, so angry, she thought the top of her head was going to explode. With a jerk, she shrugged his arm off her shoulders. She couldn't bear for him to touch her, not when everything he'd said, everything he'd done, had been a lie.

He didn't care about her, not even a little. He couldn't.

When she looked at him, her eyes were blue flames. "Why didn't you tell me?"

What was going on? "Tell you what?"

How could he sit there and make her tell him? How could he put her through this? And how could he have done this to her?

A sob rose in her throat. No, not this time. The tears weren't allowed to come this time. They weren't going to embarrass her in front of him any further. She had given herself to him on every level and he had held himself back from her, like a stranger. All he had shared with her was his body.

She didn't want half measures. If it couldn't be all, it would be nothing.

Her voice was dangerously still as she said, "Why didn't you tell me how you really knew Dr. Benjamin when I asked you?"

Warning signs shot up, but he ignored them. He'd come too far in this direction to retrace his steps. He watched her face as he answered cautiously, "I told you, he was my ex-father-in-law's doctor."

He was still lying to her. She could have hit him. "Then what is he doing operating on Katie?" She didn't want to yell, to give him the satisfaction of seeing how deeply he had hurt her, but the momentum in her voice, once activated, began to escalate. "*Why* is he operating on Katie?"

Holding on to the sheet, she wrapped it around herself as she rose to her knees over him, indignation and fury in her eyes. "That was the hospital, calling to confirm Katie's operation. What operation? What's wrong with her?"

He hated being put in this position, hated her knowing that he had lied to her. "Why didn't you give me the telephone?"

Was that all he had to say to her? He'd cut out her heart and he wanted to know why she hadn't conducted proper telephone etiquette?

She slammed her palm against his chest in frustration. "They didn't *ask* for you, and that's not an answer. Why were you keeping this from me?"

He fell back on the very first reason he had. "This doesn't concern you."

He couldn't have found a better weapon to use against her than if he had deliberately tried.

Her eyes widened. "Doesn't concern me? Doesn't concern me?" she repeated incredulously. "I *care* about her." Couldn't he understand that? Didn't he know? "Somewhere along the line, I started taking being called Mommy seriously."

And then it became clear to her.

"Oh, I see." She raised her chin defiantly, fervently wishing she could pull a cloak around herself and disappear. "I'm good enough to sleep with, good enough to take money from, but not good enough to be let into your life, is that it?"

His pride stung at the mention of money. "No, that's not it and you know it," he shouted at her.

"I don't know anything of the kind," she countered. "And as for the money, I guess that was our bargain, wasn't it? Two years of your life for two hundred thousand dollars. That comes to $273.97 a day. That's pretty cheap, really. Maybe you should charge time and a half for the nights."

He had no defense against the hurt in her eyes, nor against the guilt he felt knowing he was responsible for putting it there.

His voice was toneless. "It's not like that, Courtney."

Then why wasn't he trying to explain? There had to be more. He owed her that, owed her an explanation.

"Then what is it like, John? Tell me. You've got too much pride to take money from someone. If you didn't, you would have gotten it from Diane in the divorce settlement."

She knew she'd struck a nerve the moment she'd said it. His eyes had darkened at the mention of her name. "I never took a penny from Diane."

That's what didn't make any sense. "But you were willing to sell yourself into servitude for two years to me. Why?"

What was the use? "To pay for Katie's operation," he finally admitted. John dragged air into his lungs. She might as well know the rest of it. "Katie was born with a congenital condition. She has something called a Ventricular Septal Defect. In layman's language, there's a small hole in her heart, in the lower chambers between the left and right ventricle. She can function fairly well with it, but she gets tired when she plays, very tired."

It made sense now, she thought, the way Gabriel had hovered over his daughter, cautioning her, wanting he to rest. But he could have told her. *Should* have told her.

"And Dr. Benjamin *was* Diane's father's doctor. He was called in when Katie was born. He's been her cardiologist ever since. He's been waiting for her to become strong enough to have bypass surgery so that he could repair the hole. It wasn't supposed to be for another year, but lately," he said, his voice becoming tight, "Katie's been getting more tired more often. He thought it best to hurry the timetable along."

Courtney covered her mouth, devastated by the news that Katie was ill, and devastated by the fact that he thought he could keep it from her. "And you didn't think enough of me to tell me?"

"It's not the kind of thing you toss out in casual conversation," he snapped in frustration.

But it was the kind of thing you shared with someone you loved. "Didn't you think I might notice when she didn't come down to breakfast one morning that something was wrong?" she shouted back at him, blinking back her tears. "How could you have thought that she could go in for that kind of surgery without me knowing?''

John reached for her, then let his hand drop to his side. He was at a loss how to handle this.

''Look, I've been dealing with things on my own for so long, it just got to be a habit.'' He tried to make more sense of it than that. As he spoke, reasons began to gel that even he hadn't been conscious of. ''Diane left me because she couldn't deal with it, couldn't deal with the idea of a sick child. Maybe on some level, I thought if I told you, you'd have the same reaction. That you'd want to terminate our 'arrangement.' I honestly don't know. I do know that I didn't want Katie to feel rejected again. And she would have if you pulled back. So it was easier not telling you than risking having you leave.''

She couldn't believe she was hearing this. After the past week, didn't he know her better than this? Hadn't he taken the time to get to know the woman he was making love with?

''You think that little of me?''

He shook his head. Katie came first. He was all she had. If he didn't think of her, no one would. ''I didn't know what to think.''

''I guess that's obvious.'' Sheet tucked around her, Courtney rose from the bed. She didn't know how to deal with him, with what he had done to them. ''I have to take a shower.''

There was a wall between them again. And he had supplied the bricks. ''Courtney—''

She didn't trust herself to look at him. ''I don't want to talk to you right now. I don't want to say something in the heat of the moment that one of us might regret. Please, just go.''

She heard the door close as she walked into the bathroom.

Chapter Fifteen

He was in her room when she came out of the shower.

The shower had been a long one. Every surface in the pink-and-gray tiled bathroom behind her was deeply fogged, covered with a thick layer of mist that reminded her of her own tears. She had stood there while the shower head pulsated water at her, trying to sort out her emotions.

She was as confused and hurt now as she had been hundreds of gallons of water ago.

Seeing him in her room didn't help.

Courtney stopped toweling her hair. Hadn't he even bothered to listen? "I thought I said——"

He wasn't going to let her throw him out until he said what he'd returned to say. "I know what you said, but I wanted to say I was sorry."

She took a deep breath and then exhaled slowly. The word came very easily to more than a few people she knew. But not for John. It had taken a great deal for him to say that to her.

Courtney pressed her lips together and nodded. "It's a start, I suppose."

She draped the towel around her neck, running her fingers through her tangled, wet hair. Barefoot, denuded of makeup, she was still the most desirable, the most beautiful, woman he'd ever seen.

"But it doesn't change what's happened," she went on. "You lied to me, excluded me. You make me feel that everything that has happened between us happened because I was your—" She searched for something to cut to the heart of the matter. Nothing pithy came to mind. Words were failing her. Everything, it seemed, was failing her. "Your piggy bank," she finally retorted in frustration.

He hated her feeling that way about the relationship that had unfolded between them. The only thing he had done in exchange for money was to marry her. Everything else had happened for reasons that had nothing to do with money. She had to know that.

"Making love with you wasn't part of the deal," he reminded her.

She'd never bargained on that. Never bargained on falling in love with the man she'd chosen only to fulfill a requirement. "No," she agreed quietly. "It wasn't."

He drew closer to her. There were a great many things in his life that had gone wrong, but at all costs, he didn't want this to be one of them. "And I wouldn't have made love to you if I didn't...feel something for you," he finally admitted. "No amount of money in the world would have made me prostitute myself that far."

Her head jerked up and something hard entered her eyes. "That far," she repeated.

He could have kicked himself. It wasn't what he meant. "Poor choice of words."

She didn't think so. Maybe his subconscious had only let slip what he actually felt in his heart. "Telling choice of words."

He opened his mouth to deny it, and then stopped. With effort, he examined his conscience.

"Maybe," he relented. When she turned away, he caught her by the wrist and turned her around. He forced her to look at him. There was more, and she had to hear it. "Because in the beginning, that's what I felt I was doing. But I was doing it for Katie, not for the money." He searched her face, her eyes, looking for something, a spark that told him she understood. "Haven't you ever loved anyone so much that you would have done anything for them? Done anything to save them?"

She thought of her father. She would have traded half her life to give him just one more week of his own. Then she thought of Katie, and how she felt as she had listened to John explain her condition.

"Yes."

Hope began to build. "Well?"

She couldn't forgive him, not yet. It wasn't that simple for her. It would have been simple only if she hadn't cared. "Like I said, it's a start." She closed her eyes and thought. There was more to consider than just their relationship. Or the end of it.

"The operation's Friday, right?" When she opened her eyes to look at him, John nodded. "All right, then, let's fill now until Friday with as much happiness as she can stand."

He didn't leave. "She'll want you there."

"I intend to be there," Courtney replied crisply, then measured out her words as she added, "And for Katie's sake, we'll pretend to be a family." There was no humor in her eyes when she laughed at the thought. "Always pretending for one reason or another, aren't we?"

He wanted to hold her, to make her understand how really sorry he was. To ask her to hold him and promise that everything would be all right.

But he didn't. He just remained where he was, an insurmountable distance away. "Maybe some of us are just pretending to pretend and we don't know it."

She wanted to believe him but was afraid to. She'd been hurt enough for one day.

For one lifetime.

"Pretty eloquent for an engineer."

He didn't think of himself as that anymore. It, along with Diane, was all in his past. "Carpenters have their moments." John started for the door. "I'll let you get dressed."

She merely nodded, not trusting her voice any longer.

He left the room just in time. If he'd stayed, he would have seen the tears.

Courtney put everything else in her life on hold, canceling long-standing obligations and sending Mandy in her place to chair a meeting of the foundation's board. She gave no explanations, except to Mandy. And Mandy promised not to tell.

She tried her hardest. So did John. For Katie's sake, they were an inseparable family unit for the next five days. They went to amusement parks, to the movies, to the zoo and even to a children's play at the Orange Coast Performing Arts Center. A few discreet calls to the right people had yielded front-row seats at the sold-out performance. It had been worth the effort to see the look on Katie's face as she watched the performance. The one on John's as he watched his daughter laugh and applaud was a bonus.

And gradually, with Katie between them, somewhere along the line the laughter became a little less forced, the words a little less strained, the feelings a little more intimate.

You would have almost believed, Courtney thought as Sam, the chauffeur, drove them to Harris Memorial Hospital early Friday morning, that they were a real family instead of two actors putting on a play for a little girl's benefit.

She looked at Katie, her heart aching. The little girl had become so very dear to her in such an incredibly short amount of time.

To think, she'd sat there at the fund-raiser, blissfully ignorant, thinking how she would feel if it was Katie whose life was threatened by a dangerous medical condition. Well, now she knew. And it hurt like hell.

They were making good time. Too good. They were almost there. There was very little traffic on Newport Boulevard at this hour in the morning. Courtney stared out the window. The fog, rolling in from the harbor, hadn't had time to lift yet. It was crouching all around them, encircling them. The way it encircled her heart, threatening to break it in two.

John had wanted to drive this morning, but she had insisted on the limousine. He was in no condition to concentrate on the road. She could see it in his eyes. He was afraid.

So was she.

It was all she could do to keep the fear from immobilizing her. To keep it a secret from Katie. She didn't want the little girl being afraid, too. Four was too young to have fear as a playmate.

It was only later, as you grew older, that it rode beside you, placing an icy hand on your heart, Courtney thought. Nothing was ever guaranteed in life, certainly not the outcome of a delicate surgery, even when the doctor performing it was as renowned for his skill as Dr. Benjamin was.

And Katie was so small....

She couldn't let herself think about the consequences. Instead, she looked at Katie. To Katie's delight, John had purposely left behind her loathed car seat when she had gotten into the limousine. She looked at him in wonder as he strapped her in with only a seat belt.

"Did you forget?" she asked.

He shook his head. "No, I didn't forget. You're a big girl now, Katie. You can ride without one."

He knew how much this meant to her. It was the last favor he could grant her before she went for her surgery. He got in beside her and nodded at the chauffeur. Sam started the vehicle.

"Nothing's going to happen to you as long as you're between us."

He'd exchanged looks with Courtney and she had given him the most positive smile she could manage. They both prayed that what he'd said would prove to be true.

So now Katie sat between them, her beloved Mr. Softy on her lap and her hand in Courtney's as she talked about all that she was going to do once she returned home from the hospital.

Courtney thought her heart was going to break, but somehow she found a way to nod and say the right things. And silently offer up every prayer and fragment of a prayer that she knew.

Arriving all too soon, John got out and led the way

to the hospital entrance. He began to walk to the left as soon as they passed through the electronic doors.

Courtney laid a hand on his arm. "Where are you going?"

He was having difficulty functioning. "To the preadmit desk. I've got papers—"

Courtney shook her head. "I already took care of that." She'd called the day before, making new arrangements. "She's going to have the best of everything. I reserved a private tower suite for her and there'll be a private duty nurse by her bed around the clock until she's ready to come home."

He knew she meant well, knew he was being unreasonable to resent the intrusion. But the fear he was grappling with overrode common sense and restraint.

"You had no right to do that without asking me first." For Katie's sake, he tried to keep his voice low. "She's my daughter, Courtney."

"No," Courtney corrected, looking at the small face. She couldn't bear to look at John's. Even after what he'd said, the way he'd apologized on Sunday, he was shutting her out again. "She's ours."

If she lived forever, she would always remember the love she saw in Katie's eyes as the girl looked up at her that morning.

They remained with Katie in her pre-op room for as long as they could, trying not to get in each other's space. But then, it came time to allow Katie to be taken away. A nurse began to give them directions to the surgical waiting area.

Courtney stopped her. "I know the way. I've been here before."

They walked down the long, carpeted hallway in painful, self-imposed silence, hardly seeing the other people they passed. The waiting area, when they arrived, was mercifully empty.

Although not as empty as they felt.

Hugging Katie's rabbit to her, Courtney looked around the room. There was a huge window on one side, overlooking the boats in the harbor. Great pains had been taken to make the room as comfortable and soothing as possible.

Unable to sit, she ran her hand along the back of one of the sofas.

"You know, my father donated the money to refurbish this room. The first time I sat in it, it was to wait for news about his condition." Even now, the memory brought fresh tears to her eyes. Courtney wiped them away with the tips of her fingers. "Hospitals always make me maudlin."

This wasn't the time to dwell on her own feelings. She looked at John's stony expression. "She's going to be all right," she whispered.

He didn't believe it. He was bracing himself for the worst. "Yeah."

Needing to move, to do something, Courtney thought of the cafeteria in the basement. "I'm going down to get us something to eat." She knew it was useless to ask him to come along. "Do you want anything special?"

He shoved his hands into his pockets as he looked out the window. "No."

He couldn't just go on torturing himself like this. It wasn't helping Katie. And it was destroying her to watch. "John, the operation's going to take at least eight hours. You didn't eat anything at breakfast—"

He didn't even look in her direction. He couldn't. If

he didn't keep a tight rein on what was going on inside, he was going to lose it.

"I said no," he snapped.

Courtney turned away. "No it is."

Courtney tried to take her time getting back to the waiting room, but she couldn't. Even as she left John, she'd wanted to rush back, to make him talk to her. To tear down this artificial barrier between them with her bare hands. They were both involved here, both worried about Katie. This wasn't the time to retreat to separate, inaccessible corners, no matter what their other grievances were. They needed each other to get through this.

But how could she convince him of that? How could she make him reach out to take the hand she offered?

He was still standing by the window, staring out at the harbor, when she returned. She wondered if he actually saw anything.

Courtney removed the two paper cups filled with coffee from the cardboard tray she'd carried up and placed them on the coffee table. A cellophane-wrapped sandwich joined them.

"I brought you back some coffee and a sandwich. Ham and cheese," she added impotently. He still wasn't looking at her. "On rye."

He didn't want her doing things for him. He didn't want anything, except for Katie to open her eyes again and call him Daddy. "I said I wasn't hungry."

"Maybe later," she murmured. Courtney folded the tray in half and threw it in the trash.

He couldn't stand this, he thought. Ever since last night, a kaleidoscope of memories had been whirling around in his brain. He was afraid that they were all setting siege to him because, soon, memories would be all he had left of his daughter.

He needed to know she was going to be all right. Needed someone to assure him that his daughter was going to survive.

He needed someone.

God, he wanted to reach out to Courtney, but he just didn't know how. Didn't know what to say, how to start. So he didn't.

Courtney watched him. He hadn't moved a muscle since she'd returned. Probably since she'd left. His shoulders were rigid. Something so rigid was destined to break sooner or later.

She didn't know how to prevent that, she only knew she wanted to. More than anything else, she wanted to.

But he wouldn't talk to her, wouldn't let her in and she didn't know how to try anymore.

At a loss, Courtney sat down on the sofa and took the coffee cup in her hand. Prying off the opaque lid, she slowly sipped coffee she didn't taste, and waited.

"You didn't have to do that, you know."

She looked up, startled. For a second, she thought she'd imagined John's voice. He hadn't said anything in more than half an hour.

"What? Bring you up a sandwich?" It was the first thing she could think of, and the last thing she'd talked about. The sandwich was still sitting there, untouched, as was his coffee. "It gave me something to do."

He turned from the window, his face an unreadable mask etched in anguish. "No, I mean take care of the hospital bill."

Were they back to that again? That was the least of

what she could do. Tired of hurting, of waiting, her temper flared.

"Hell, what else is money good for?" She replaced the empty cup on the table and turned to face him. "That's why you agreed to this marriage, wasn't it? So I'm giving you a bonus. Because I love her. And she's not going to lack for anything."

It was his pride talking, not him. It was all he had left to hang on to. "Our bargain was for a set amount of money, Courtney. It wouldn't be right to ask for more."

Her nerves, frayed, snapped now. "Right?" she echoed in disbelief. "We're way past right and wrong here." It was an effort not to shout at him. "She's not some exercise in a math book, damn it. Get so much, pay so much," she said in a singsong voice. "She's a little girl. A little girl I love a great deal."

She was off the sofa now, and ready to go a couple of rounds with him. Maybe it would make them both feel better. Anything was better than just sitting here and waiting in silence.

"Do you really think I could just put a check on the table and walk away from her? From both of you?"

Was she telling him what he wanted—no, needed—to hear, after everything that had been said? "I—"

Courtney burrowed a finger into his chest. "Yeah, you. Mr. Personality. I can't just walk away from you, though I should. God help me, I thought I was a lot smarter than this, but I guess it takes me a while to learn things. No matter what you think of me, what you feel—or rather, don't feel—for me, I will always be there for Katie. And if you need anything, well, maybe I'll be there for you, too."

The angry tears in her eyes told him everything he wanted to know. "Courtney—"

When he reached for her, she backed away. She didn't want gestures he didn't mean. "If you want to apologize, you don't have to."

But he took her into his arms, not to comfort her, but to comfort himself. It was a homecoming for him. For both of them.

He held her close, burying his face in her hair. "Don't leave, Courtney."

It wasn't until she played back his words in her head that she actually heard him. Courtney pulled back to look up into his face. "Weren't you just listening? I have no intentions of leaving."

It was only when he repeated it that she understood. "Don't leave me."

She could have cried.

And did.

For a long time, they just stood there, holding on to each other, supporting each other as best they could. Finally, John drew away, holding her at arm's length. It was time, he thought, to let go of the silence. It was time to tell her. Everything.

"When I first married Diane, it was like walking into a fairy tale. She was crazy about me, or so she said," he tacked on. He'd been too in love with the idea of having someone to love to see past the lies. "And I believed her. Wanted desperately to believe her. You see, I'd never had anyone love me before. Ever."

That sounded impossible. "But your parents—"

He cut her off. "I never knew my father. My mother, too young, she claimed, to be tied down with a brat, abandoned me with her brother and sister-in-law when I was three." His mouth twisted at the memory of his aunt and uncle. He bore them no ill will, nor any love, either. Not anymore. "Two very God-fearing people who wouldn't have dreamed of turning me out because that just wasn't allowed. But there was nothing in the rule book they were following about loving a kid, either, so they didn't.''

It had taken him a while to come to terms with that. He'd always thought that, somehow, it had been his fault. His fault his mother left. His fault his uncle and aunt couldn't love him. When he was younger, he hadn't realized that some people were just what they were.

"I left home the day I graduated high school. I could hear their sighs of relief as I walked out the door."

The look in his eyes told her that the pain wasn't completely erased, no matter what he said. "Oh, John, I'm so sorry."

He didn't hear her, refused to hear the pity in her voice. He'd come this far without it and he would continue. There were worse lives.

John shrugged. "I put myself through college, doing whatever it took to earn enough money to pay for books and tuition. I moved around a lot, from place to place, just ahead of the landlord. Food was optional."

He saw the horror in her eyes. It hadn't been so bad at the time. In a way, it had been an adventure. "Hey, it builds character. Although if I had actually had it, maybe I could have seen through Diane. I would have been able to realize that all she wanted was a diversion, something to amuse herself with for a while. Someone to aggravate her parents with." He could almost laugh about it now. Almost. "And I did. Oh, boy, did I. They hated me. They threw her a party the day she announced she wanted a divorce. Except that by then, she was pregnant."

Diane had called him, upset, confused, angry, not knowing what to do. He'd talked her into having the baby. Technically, Katie was his from the very first moment.

"So we stuck it out for a while and I guess I hoped that things would work out in the long run. But they didn't."

He paused, taking a breath, steeling himself from the memory. "When they found out Katie had a hole in her heart, Diane really fell apart. She blamed me for 'saddling' her with this baby and said she didn't want to see her. She calmed down eventually and actually tried being a mother for a while. That lasted all of three months. She said the baby's crying made her nervous. That she wasn't cut out to take care of a child, especially not a sick one."

Looking back, he wondered how he could have ever thought himself in love with such a vain, self-centered woman.

"This time, the divorce went through. I got custody, completely uncontested. Her parents were even willing to negotiate a settlement—provided I never approached them or Diane again. I told them what they could do with their money and left with my daughter."

This time, when she put her arms around him, he didn't draw away.

"We got by for a while. I had a job with a good firm by then. But in order to keep a job, you have to show up regularly, and Katie needed a series of operations." He sighed. "There were complications. I had to stay home to take care of her. I won't bore you with the details, but the upshot of it was that I wound up with two mortgages on the house and no source of income. The firm said they hated to let me go, but they had no choice.

"That's when I fell back on carpentry. It's what I did

in college and it gave me the opportunity to keep Katie with me. I wanted her around as much as I could. About a year ago, I read that Diane had been killed in an auto accident. She'd been drinking.'' He recited it as if it was news about a stranger.

Still, the woman had once been his wife. "I'm sorry," Courtney said.

He shook his head. "Any feelings I might have had for her died a long time ago. I don't think the woman I was in love with really existed, except in my imagination.'' He took Courtney's hands in his, searching her face for some indication of what she felt. He'd never put himself on the line this way before. "So there you have it. The uncondensed, unabridged version of my life."

She knew what it must have taken for him to tell her. "Thank you."

He didn't understand. "For what?"

"For letting me in."

He smiled into her face. It was he who should be thanking her. "I had no choice. I love you."

As soon as he said it, she knew it was true. "I know. You just proved it.'' Her heart swelled as she lost herself in his arms.

Chapter Sixteen

The surgeon had barely entered the waiting room before Courtney was at his side.

"How is she, Doctor?"

Darel Benjamin smiled before answering, savoring the moment. He'd just spent the past eight hours and twenty-one minutes trying to make certain that Katie Gabriel had a future. And he had succeeded. Others might argue the point, but for him, there was no greater sense of accomplishment than being able to hand tomorrow to a patient.

"She came through it like a trouper." He looked at John and recognized a haunted look he was all too familiar with. "She's going to be just fine," he assured John. "No incidents, no problems. Textbook surgery with a model patient."

Thank you, God, Courtney thought, squeezing John's hand. "When can we see her?" she asked eagerly.

The doctor pulled off his blue surgical cap, freeing the shock of chestnut hair. Exhaustion lined his face. "They're going to be transporting her in a few minutes. It'll take a while to get everything into place. She'll be in CCU for a few days. The cardiac care unit," he clarified for Courtney's benefit. "It's down the hall. The signs'll get you there."

He laid a hand on John's shoulder. The rigidity was beginning to fade. "You and I already know what a resilient constitution Katie has. She's going to be up and running around before you know it." The surgeon looked down at his gown. "Now if you'll excuse me, I'm going to get cleaned up and get some coffee in my system before I go into withdrawal. I'll be around to see her late this evening," he promised as he left.

"Thank you, Doctor," Courtney called after him.

He stopped in the doorway. "Hey, I'm as happy about this as you are." He looked at the two of them. "Well, almost."

John took Courtney into his arms. They held on to each other for a long time, too relieved, too numbed with joy, to say anything. They didn't have to.

Finally, after what seemed like an eternity, John released her. "Thank you for being here with me."

She wished he wouldn't make it sound as if she were on some goodwill mission. Or as if she were Mandy, who had stopped by the hospital earlier to sit with them for a few hours. She was as involved in this as he was. "As if I could have been anywhere else."

He was beginning to really believe that. "Hey, you know, I'm suddenly hungry."

She looked at the remains of the sandwich she'd brought him hours ago. When he hadn't wanted it, she'd begun to nibble at it nervously until most of it was gone. She didn't even remember tasting it.

"Well, I ate the sandwich," she said ruefully.

Eating the corner that was left, he tossed away the wrapper. "Benjamin said they'd be a while setting things up. Do you want to go get something to eat?"

She couldn't eat. Her stomach was still tied up in knots that were only now beginning to loosen. Food held no appeal to her. "No, that's all right, I'll wait here."

"Be right back," he promised. And then he was gone, hurrying to the bank of elevators in the rear of the hospital.

When he returned, Courtney wasn't in the waiting room. There was another couple occupying the area. Young, their faces creased with concern, they looked as worried as Courtney and he had been just a little while ago. Both turned and looked at him hopefully when he entered. Realizing he wasn't who they were waiting for, they looked away.

Confused, John rested the cardboard tray he'd brought up from the cafeteria on the table. "Excuse me, did you see a blond woman in here, about thirty?"

The man didn't answer, but the woman nodded. A handkerchief was twisted in her hands. "She left a few minutes ago. It might have been half an hour. I don't know. I'm sorry."

He understood. His mind had been in the same fog less than an hour ago.

"Thanks." And then he stopped just shy of the threshold. It wasn't his way to intrude into anyone else's life, but today was different.

"Don't worry, it's going to be all right," he assured them. "This is a really great hospital."

As if they were one, the couple nodded their gratitude for the words of support.

John looked down at the tray he was carrying. He'd bought two more coffees and two sandwiches for them. He felt a little foolish carrying it around with him now as he looked up and down the hall. Where could she have gone?

And then he realized that she had taken Mr. Softy, and it came to him.

Reading the signs that were posted at every turn of the hall, he found his way to the CCU corridor. Steel gray double doors yawned open as he approached the threshold, urging him to enter the sunny corridor.

The walls within the CCU area were painted in mute pastels and framed paintings hung here and there to highlight the colors. It seemed a place where a person was destined to get well.

A nurse posted at a desk before the recovery area cubicles gave him a friendly smile. Looking at the tray in his hands, she shook her head. "You can't bring that in there, sir."

"Yes, I know." He placed the tray on her desk. She could eat what was on it, he didn't care. Right now, John felt like buying lunch for the entire hospital staff. "I'm John Gabriel. My little girl—"

The name was fresh in her mind. "They just brought her in. Your wife's already with her. Ten minutes," she warned, a trim, clear polished nail tapping the sign posted on the side of the desk. Patients were allowed only ten-minute visits every hour. There was a two-person limit per cubicle. "Fifteen, tops," she added, her smile widening. "First cubicle on your left."

He thanked her and went in.

Your wife's already with her.

It had a good sound. A comforting sound. Maybe it was the euphoria of the moment, but for the first time in his life, John felt really whole. If it was euphoria, he hoped it would never fade.

And then he saw her, standing next to Katie's bed, holding the sleeping child's hand in her own. Mr. Softy was tucked in beside Katie. Courtney was stroking her forehead and saying something to her. He felt as if he was intruding.

He couldn't draw away. Like a magnet, the scene pulled him in.

Courtney seemed unaware of his presence. "And when you get well, honey, I'll take you anywhere you want to go." Courtney paused, trying to gather her thoughts into something that resembled coherence. "There's Disney World." It was the first place that came to mind. "I bet you haven't been to Florida yet. Every child should go to Disney World, at least once."

It was hard to talk with tears tightening her throat. But for once they were good tears. She felt so very grateful.

"I want to give you everything, baby. The way you've given everything to me." Careful not to disturb any of the myriad tubes attached to the various monitors, Courtney leaned forward and very gently pressed a kiss to Katie's forehead.

"I love you, Katie. I know I haven't said the words out loud to you, but I do. I love you very much. And your big lug of a father, too. Even if he can be dumber than rain sometimes."

"Dumber than rain?" John whispered, moving beside her. "Where do you get these expressions?"

She looked up at him, too emotionally overcome to be indignant at being caught, or to even be startled. She hadn't the energy. It had all been drained from her.

"You're eavesdropping again, Gabriel. This is a private conversation."

He grinned. She'd called him by his last name again, but this time, he knew it no longer was a sign of the distance between them, but an indication of how far they had come.

"A one-way conversation, as usual. You don't let people get in a word edgewise, do you?"

Courtney looked down at Katie. "She can get in all the words she wants to once she's awake. I'll be listening," she promised.

Seeing her like this, with Katie, made him come to a decision. Or maybe it just rubber-stamped a decision that had been made for him on some higher plane from the very beginning.

"Speaking of listening, I'd like to talk something over with you. Now that all of Katie's bills are being taken care of and Parsons has set the wheels in motion for your inheritance to be transferred, maybe we should discuss our arrangement again."

She looked at him. He couldn't be choosing this moment to pull away. She refused to believe it of him. "You mean, renegotiate?"

It wasn't exactly the word he'd had in mind, but it would do. "Well, yes. Specifically, about the time. Originally, you said two years, right?"

Where *was* he going with this? Courtney turned to face him. "Right."

Though he thought he was certain of her answer, he suddenly felt a little unsteady. "And the timetable's been moved up, so to speak."

"So to speak," she repeated cautiously. Her eyes searched his face. There was a glimmer in his eyes, but no clear answers. "Are you asking to get out?"

He wasn't sure how much longer he could keep a straight face. How much longer he could refrain from just sweeping her into his arms and telling her that he loved her with every fiber of his being.

"No, just to have things labeled a little more clearly."

"Such as?"

"Well—" he drew the word out "—you mentioned that once everything was settled, we would get a divorce after a decent length of time had lapsed."

She vaguely remembered uttering something to that effect—in another lifetime. "Yes?"

He placed his hands around her waist. It was then that she knew there was nothing to worry about. Ever again. "Define decent length of time."

She smiled into his eyes. Two could play this game. "How about the twelfth?"

For a glimmer of a moment, she had him a little uneasy again. "Of?"

"Never?" It was a question, not an answer, and she was aware of holding her breath as she asked.

He blew out the one he'd been unconsciously holding. His hands slid up from her waist to her back and he pulled her closer. "I know why they keep you on as head of the foundation's board."

Courtney arched a playful eyebrow. "Because my father started the foundation?"

"No, because you drive a hard bargain—"

"I can change that date—"

"Let me finish. Hard, but fair." He brushed a kiss to her temple. "Very fair."

She could feel her knees beginning to melt already. "Then you like the twelfth of never?"

"Very much." He kissed her again, this time skimming her eyelids and her cheek before lightly brushing her lips. "But with my luck, it'll come all too soon."

Her arms twined around his neck as she pressed her body to his. It was where she belonged. Where they both belonged. "Don't bet the farm on it."

He shook his head. "Not even a single pony."

At the mention of the word, Katie made a sound and stirred, though she went on sleeping.

"She can't be too asleep if she can hear that," Courtney noted.

The laughter in the tiny cubicle was filled with love, as was the kiss that followed.

* * * * *

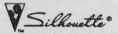

Take 4 bestselling love stories FREE

Plus get a FREE surprise gift!

Special Limited-time Offer

Mail to Silhouette Reader Service™

3010 Walden Avenue
P.O. Box 1867
Buffalo, N.Y. 14240-1867

YES! Please send me 4 free Silhouette Special Edition® novels and my free surprise gift. Then send me 6 brand-new novels every month, which I will receive months before they appear in bookstores. Bill me at the low price of $3.34 each plus 25¢ delivery and applicable sales tax, if any.* That's the complete price and a savings of over 10% off the cover prices—quite a bargain! I understand that accepting the books and gift places me under no obligation ever to buy any books. I can always return a shipment and cancel at any time. Even if I never buy another book from Silhouette, the 4 free books and the surprise gift are mine to keep forever.

235 BPA A3UV

Name	(PLEASE PRINT)	
Address	Apt. No.	
City	State	Zip

This offer is limited to one order per household and not valid to present Silhouette Special Edition® subscribers. *Terms and prices are subject to change without notice. Sales tax applicable in N.Y.

USPED-696

©1990 Harlequin Enterprises Limited

SHARON SALA

Continues the twelve-book
series—36 HOURS—
in October 1997
with Book Four

FOR HER EYES ONLY

The storm was over. The mayor was dead. Jessica Hanson
had an aching head...and sinister visions of murder.
And only one man was willing to take her seriously—
Detective Stone Richardson. He knew that unlocking
Jessica's secrets would put him in danger, but the rugged
cop had never expected to fall for her, too. Danger he could
handle. But love...?

For Stone and Jessica and *all* the residents of Grand Springs,
Colorado, the storm-induced blackout was just the beginning
of 36 Hours that changed *everything!* You won't want to miss a
single book.

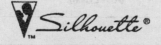

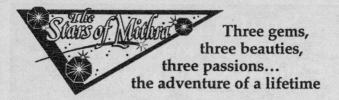

Silhouette®

SPECIAL EDITION™

COMING NEXT MONTH

#1135 WHITE WOLF—Lindsay McKenna
That Special Woman!
Hardened corporate raider Dain Phillips turned to mystical medicine woman Erin Wolf for a "miracle" cure. But he never expected to care so deeply for Erin—or that her spiritual healing would forever alter him body and soul!

#1136 THE RANCHER AND THE SCHOOLMARM—
Penny Richards
Switched at Birth
Schoolteacher Georgia Williams was stunned when her fiancé passed her in the airport, got attacked and suffered amnesia. How would she handle the revelation that this riveting man who stole her heart was *not* her groom-to-be—but instead his long-lost identical twin?

#1137 A COWBOY'S TEARS—Anne McAllister
Code of the West
Mace and Jenny Nichols had the *perfect* marriage—until Mace discovered some sad news. Jenny was determined to convince her brooding cowboy of her unfaltering love—and that there was more than one way to capture their dreams....

#1138 THE PATERNITY TEST—Pamela Toth
Powerful Nick Kincaid could handle anything—except his mischievous twins. His new nanny, Cassie Wainright, could handle everything—except her attraction to Nick. Now Cassie was pregnant, and Nick was being put to the *ultimate* test.

#1139 HUSBAND: BOUGHT AND PAID FOR—Laurie Paige
Fearing for her life, heiress Jessica Lockhart hired P.I. Brody Smith—and then proposed marriage. Her aloof bodyguard agreed to a platonic union, but that didn't mean the lovely lady had the right to wiggle her way into his heart.

#1140 MOUNTAIN MAN—Doris Rangel
Gloria Pellman was a single mom, raising her young son, Jamey—alone, thank you very much! She didn't need a husband! But when Hank Mason rescued them from his rugged mountain, Jamey discovered a friend...and Gloria discovered her heart was in danger!

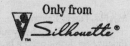